MACL

The forceful Adam Maclean represented everything Lucy had come to Brazil to fight—so-called 'progress' encroaching on and destroying the Indians' simple civilisation—and she hated him and all he was doing. But what would happen if her hate should turn to desire—as she suspected it so easily could?

MACLEAN'S WOMAN

BY

ANN COOPER

MILLS & BOON LIMITED

15-16 BROOK'S MEWS
LONDON W1A 1DR

First published 1981
Australian copyright 1981
Philippine copyright 1981
This edition 1981

© Ann Cooper 1981

ISBN 0 263 73580 x

Set in Monophoto Baskerville 11 on 12 pt.

Made and printed in Great Britain by Richard Clay (The Chaucer Press) Ltd, Bungay, Suffolk

CHAPTER ONE

'I want to speak to Adam Maclean,' Lucy repeated fiercely. 'What do you mean, *maybe* he isn't here? I *know* he's here. I haven't travelled fifty miles through this blessed jungle just for the sake of my health!' She stared at the small, wiry mechanic fellow who had just crawled from under a Land Rover. *Land Rovers*, was it? These people certainly knew how to travel in style.

The man wiped his hands slowly on an oily rag. He was as brown as a walnut, and just as tough and hard, Lucy guessed. When he spoke again it was with a sharp Cockney accent.

'But the Gov'nor's pretty fussy who he sees,' he had the cheek to tell her. 'Maybe he'll speak to you,' he shrugged, 'and maybe he won't.'

'Have you any idea who you're speaking to?' Lucy persevered, drawing herself upright and looking incensed.

'You're not going to tell me it's Robinson Crusoe and Man Friday,' he quipped, not in the least impressed that an English girl and a Brazilian native had strolled into his camp.

One or two people laughed. Lucy saw other men appearing out of the jungle, or from a truck. They were all lean and brown, some of them were leering at her and she realised they probably hadn't seen a woman for weeks.

What a mess! Everything was going dreadfully wrong. And she was so hot and exhausted and the wretched man was being deliberately awkward. But they probably did look an incongruous pair; a pint-sized blonde, her tumbling curls in bunches, and a tall, dark Amerindian, naked except for decorative arm and leg bands and a leather thong holding his knife. He didn't understand the conversation, but he knew that Lucy was distressed. His hand moved towards his belt, but as she touched his arm and tried to smile, he relaxed and she turned back to the evil genie who was rubbing a spanner now, instead of a lamp.

'All I want—is to speak to Adam Maclean.' It was a great effort to keep the weariness out of her voice. It had been a long, dangerous journey, and it had been a relief finally to reach even the enemy's camp.

'I'm Maclean.' The words vibrated down Lucy's spine and she spun round. 'Did you want to see me?' the man continued calmly, yet there was something in his voice that made Lucy shiver.

They were mad—all mad—and this craggy, stern-faced creature was as bad as any of them. Didn't they realise how far she had come? He seemed no more surprised than if she had simply crossed London by train.

'Of course I want to see you. That's what I've been trying to make this—this *fellow* understand.'

He still wasn't impressed. He just stood there star-ing at her. A muscle jerked in his sunburnt cheek. It was a hard face, strong and shrewd. Butterflies danced in Lucy's stomach. Why did she suddenly feel afraid?

He motioned her behind him into a sort of canvas lean-to. It wasn't a proper tent, just an attempt to get a bit of shelter and shade. He pointed to a chair and ordered tea. Tea! What bliss. Then Lucy remembered Sam.

'We afford our guests every comfort,' she was told ambiguously. Comfort? Huh! But she had to admit that it was a relief to get out of the sun.

She flopped into the chair and took off her sunhat, wiping her damp forehead with the back of her hand. Maclean sat down and stretched out long legs across the dusty, bare floor. There was a typewriter on a folding table, a large radio receiver and a box of rolled-up maps, and some books. This was obviously his office; he would run the forward operation from here. Lucy wondered how many men were in his advance party, and how much further they had pushed civilisation towards an innocent and unprotected people.

Tea arrived, hot and strong, in tin mugs, and she was allowed to drink it and recover, in silence. She took her time, trying to plan what to say, and found herself peering at the opposition over the top of her mug. Just who was Adam Maclean? Why had *he* chosen to lead this expedition through the jungle? And why *now*, instead of next year, as had been planned? Things didn't usually happen quickly in Brazil; tomorrow would always do. So why the rush? Lucy was suspicious. What had Adam Maclean to gain by coming now? She watched as he pulled out a file from the box and began sorting through a sheaf of papers. He was wearing buff-coloured cotton trousers and an old, faded, bush-style shirt that was all buttons and tabs and gave him a harsh,

crisp, almost military look. The sleeves were rolled
up above the elbow and his arms were burnt to a
deep copper bronze. He looked as if a thousand tropical suns had radiated a pulsating strength into his
powerful body. But Lucy could sense it had done
something else as well. It was as if countless months
of danger and privation had burnt into his soul. The
dark eyes had looked strangely menacing, and the
strong, almost good-looking face was touched with
ruthlessness. When you looked at Adam Maclean
you saw danger. Was it his ability to deal with
danger—or was *he* the danger? There was a small
scar on his left cheekbone. Lucy wondered how it
had happened.

If he was aware of her scrutiny, it didn't bother
him. He was sitting there, almost relaxed, but as he
turned the pages there was firm, steady purpose in
the movement, and the dark eyes flicked down the
page with the speed and comprehension of a highly
intelligent man. Perhaps that was what had frightened her; she had been expecting a rough, blustery,
pioneering type, and had found strong, silent confidence instead.

He looked up at her suddenly and she realised she
had been staring at him all this time. She hid
behind her lashes, feeling suddenly confused.
Heavens, what was the matter with her? Maclean's
eyes met hers with unwavering coolness, then his lips
twisted and she knew that he was finding her
naïvely amusing. Let him laugh all he pleased, he
would soon find out he was wrong.

'I think it's time we got down to business, Mr
Maclean. I'm a very busy person,' she said, wiggling
her head importantly, 'and I think the sooner I tell

you who I am, and what I've come for, the sooner you'll be able to start changing your plans.'

An odd expression glowed momentarily in his eyes. He seemed to look at her again; scanning her face and slim young figure, storing away more information in his computer-like brain. His hair was thick and dark and a sun-spot danced on a curl that licked across his temple. There was a tiny rip in the canvas above his head, and as he moved the sun brought life and fire to the slim gold watch on his wrist. Lucy wondered why she should notice all these things. Was it because she had the curious feeling she had met Adam Maclean before?

She watched as he selected a loose page from the file, then swivelled round in his seat to face her. Wasn't he burning with curiosity? Didn't he want to ask what she had meant about changing his plans?

But instead of that, with aggravating calm, he leant back in his chair and crossed one long, powerful leg over the other. And when he began reading from the lined foolscap page, Lucy was so amazed she could only stare at him in silence.

'Lucy Blake,' he began, in a low, well modulated voice that expressed as much interest as if he had been reading a shopping list. 'Doing postgraduate research,' he went on unhurriedly, 'at present with the Tukama tribe, two hundred and fifty miles north-west of Kantara National Park. Been out here three months,' he interpreted, obviously calculating from the date of her arrival. 'Only white woman in the area, unmarried, twenty-one years old . . .'

'Twenty-two!' snapped Lucy, finally catching her breath.

He looked across at her over the page. 'Ah—

you've had a birthday,' he said slowly, and he had the nerve actually to pick up a pen and make an alteration.

'Yes, well, that's all very clever.' Lucy tried not to sound flustered. 'But you could have picked up all that information back at the Institute in Brasilia. I'm out here with official approval,' she reminded him sharply. 'So perhaps I can come to the point of this visit—I want to make it quite clear . . .'

He tossed the page idly back on the table and hooked one thumb over his thick, embossed leather belt. 'I don't think your visit is that much of a mystery,' he said matter-of-factly. 'I presume you've come to try and stop me excavating for the new road.' He raised one eyebrow in brief enquiry, but it wasn't really a question, *he knew*, the wretched man had known all the time.

'I see we understand each other perfectly.' Lucy gave him a crisp, bright smile. 'You can't possibly understand the damage you're doing, Mr Maclean. These Indians aren't ready for your kind of civilisation. Tribes have already been wiped out by corruption and disease. I've been told that the route you plan will go straight through the Tukamas' territory. They need space, can't you see?' If the table had been nearer she would have thumped it. 'They're hunters. It's no good expecting them to keep grazing herds and start farming. These people are only one generation away from being head-hunters. They're not equipped to cope with our modern civilisation—whatever *that's* supposed to mean,' she added bitterly.

'I completely agree.' His voice was sharper now, with a note of authority that marked him a commander of men. 'But unfortunately, Miss Blake, it's a wicked world. We can't always make nice cosy decisions. There are more sides to the question, more people involved than the very small percentage of Amerindians.'

'It's *that* sort of attitude that wipes out minority groups . . .' Lucy was on her own ground now and could face Adam Maclean with complete assurance. 'But those minority groups can teach us how to survive—we've forgotten, you see . . . Somewhere along the line we've stopped thinking about the *quality* of life. . . .'

'Yes, yes, yes,' he interrupted, waving her to immediate silence. 'That's all very well and it's an interesting story, but I don't have the time to philosophise. As I said, it's a hard life.' He stood up and unrolled one of the maps. 'According to my information,' he went on briskly, 'there shouldn't be any Indians near our route. I was told that you were in the process of moving them out. Land, apparently, has been provided for them in Kantara Park. Surely that was the whole intention of your visit to the village.'

He knew far too much for Lucy's liking. Where *had* she seen him before?

'You've got absolutely no idea what you're talking about,' she began confidently. 'Do you think I can change, in three *months*, what's been going on for thousands of years? That's the trouble with you people, you expect instant answers, instant success—and you don't have to look very far in the world to see what a shambles that kind of thinking has produced.'

'Miss Blake, you exaggerate,' he said loftily. 'The

Tukama Indians were first contacted more than thirty years ago; they've been receiving medical aid for the past fifteen to twenty years at least. I don't think anyone's expecting instant answers in this case, and you certainly wouldn't have been allowed to remain with them if they weren't considered reasonably well adjusted and trustworthy people. You shouldn't be here, Miss Blake, wasting my time and yours—you should be back with them, helping and preparing them for their journey.'

Lucy stared at him with indignation. 'And how far will it go? Huh! You tell me that. How many times will they get moved on? Their land taken away, more and more Indians squeezed into a . . . a . . . *reservation*, that's all it is, until even that will disappear when new roads are wanted . . . new technology presses forward. I'm not going back to the village, *Mr* Maclean, I'm not going to prepare them for any journey, because there isn't going to be one. And there isn't going to be a new road. Do you understand?' she practically shouted. 'Because somehow I'm going to find a way to get this whole expedition recalled!'

He rolled up the map again and sighed. 'You're wasting your time, Miss Blake, simply wasting your time.' Then his face hardened and he added with total conviction, 'The road goes *through*. Do *you* understand? It hasn't been easy and maybe it will get worse.' His eyes swept over her in disparagement. 'But I'm certainly not going to let some little blue-eyed slip of a thing stand in my way.'

Lucy glared at him, beside herself with fury, yet for once having no idea what she could do. He just stood there staring down at her, silhouetted dark and strong against the setting sun. He looked so immovable, so resilient; both in body and mind. How could she shake him from such an arrogant, self-assured pedestal? She began trembling with frustration, seething with so many things she wanted to do and say, and he simply watched her, his eyes cool and impassive, the strong mobile face totally in control. Then his gaze began to slide over her slim yet shapely body, noticing the old cotton jeans and faded tee-shirt with its distorted *Pepsi* sign blazoned across her chest. Her bunches of soft blonde curls were bouncing with righteous indignation, every inch of her was alive and glowing, her breath was uneven, and all the inner excitement seemed to please him.

'What's a nice girl like you doing in a place like this?' he suddenly purred from low and deep in his throat. And then he smiled, such an age-old, experienced, devastating smile, that Lucy felt she had been knocked into the middle of next week.

'Not very original, can't you think of anything better than that?' She rammed on her sun-hat and went to brush past him. But he caught her arm and snatched off her hat, pulling her up so tightly against him that she could hardly breathe.

'I can think of plenty of things better than this,' he taunted, enjoying himself as she squirmed against him. 'Mm, nice, isn't it?' he whispered into her hair. 'Missing your boy-friend, are you?' And then she managed to hit him and break away. But he only laughed at her with eyes that crackled with a wicked, dangerous fire.

'Give me back my hat!' she demanded, holding out her hand. Her chin was up and bright blue eyes sparkled with anger.

'How about *please*?' he dared to suggest.

'After *that* sort of behaviour you won't get a please or thank you from me!' And to her amazement he just folded up her cotton hat and slipped it into his pocket.

'When you change your mind come and see me, before you leave,' he added firmly, 'first thing in the morning.'

'You don't imagine I'm spending the night in your camp!' The sharp retort sprang to her lips, but somehow she kept the words unsaid. She didn't want to stay here, somehow she wanted to get as far away from Adam Maclean as was humanly possible. Yet she had to stay long enough to make him see sense, appeal to his better nature—if the wretched man had one. 'Your offer of hospitality overwhelms me,' she said instead. Adam Maclean looked surprised. Surprised! Huh! He hadn't seen anything yet!

The look was gone, his face was in control again, tight and rigid as he gave a brief, conclusive nod, for all the world as if he was a commanding officer dismissing his troops. 'Supper is at seven. Go and see Collison, he'll tell you where to put your things— show you which part of the river is safe to wash.' She was about to ask him which one was Collison, but he seemed to sense her question. 'Collison is the one you've already met,' he added sharply, turning back to his paperwork.

Lucy left him to it. Never mind Collison, where

was Sam? It wasn't his real name, but the nearest she had come to pronouncing it. She screwed up her eyes against the brilliant sun as it dropped behind the trees on the opposite side of the riverbank. A person could get sunstroke for not wearing a hat. Adam Maclean was a menace, and when she got back to Brasilia she would make the fact well known.

She heard a group of men laughing behind the Land Rover. If they were teasing Sam she would give them a piece of her mind. She marched over—but they weren't. There were just four or five men sitting around cleaning equipment.

'Looking for your friend?' It was the little one, Collison. Lucy nodded. 'He's down by the river, guarding your boat. Didn't seem to trust us, did he, lads?' There were surprised and innocent mutters all round. Lucy didn't blame Sam, she wouldn't have trusted this lot either. 'Want something else, did you?' she was asked, when they saw she wasn't exactly hurrying away.

'Er—Mr Maclean said you would show me where to go—where to put our hammocks—where I could have a wash . . .' She felt awkward having to ask him a favour, she had probably been a bit rude earlier on.

'Ah, well, if *Mr* Maclean asked me to do it,' the little Cockney began, winking at the others. Lucy stared into the trees while he scrambled up and dusted off his trousers. 'Perhaps I'd better warn Cook there'll be two extra to dine,' he went on in a superb butler's voice. It was just too much; Lucy giggled, then laughed outright. They all laughed, and suddenly everything was all right.

They asked her name, and all about Sam. How far had she come? How long had she been in the jungle on her own?

'I'm not on my own, there are nearly two hundred in the tribe. It's all go, you know,' she said brightly, 'I don't have time to be lonely.'

Then they told her their names, only she lost track, except for Collison, who told her to call him Jock.

'Jock? A Londoner?'

He grinned. 'It's their warped sense of humour,' he said, strolling with her down to the boat so that she could collect her things. He was dark and wiry and of a curious, indeterminate age. Yet she guessed he was a good bit older than the others. Maybe it would be a good idea to stick near him.

Sam was fishing, and when he saw Lucy his solemn face broke into a series of smiles. He was younger than she, about seventeen or eighteen, at a guess. Old enough to have grown into maturity yet still retaining some of the innocence of a boy.

She told him they would be staying the night. His Portuguese was almost as good as hers, although that wasn't saying much, and she remembered what Maclean had said about the Tukamas having been contacted by white men all those years ago. The man who organised the Kantara Park; a Brazilian, Felipe Ramirez, had been a young explorer when he had first met Sam's parents when they themselves were little more than children. Felipe had become especially fond of Sam and the boy had visited the post where the doctor had fought epidemic after epidemic, with a lack of funds and medical supplies, until the influential, wealthy doctor from Rio had become the tired yet elegant man Lucy had grown to love and respect.

It had been Felipe who had taught Sam Portuguese, and it was Felipe who had chosen the Tukama Indians when she had first written to him asking for an opportunity to continue her studies. How kind he had been—how helpful. Although not well himself, and often suffering attacks of malaria, he had travelled with her and introduced her to the village, staying for nearly a month until he decided she was really settled.

'It is still your wish to remain?' She could see him now, standing in a boat very much like this one, holding her hand, wanting to be really certain that she didn't wish to change her mind. She hadn't, although she often wondered if the wily Brazilian sensed the real reason she was out here. 'What's a nice girl like you doing in a place like this?' Adam Maclean's voice returned to taunt her, and she hardly noticed Jock and Sam beginning to unload the boat. Funny how time healed, or was it being flung into new surroundings where there were no associations, nothing to remind her? It was only during the nights now that she would think about John.

'All set, then?' Jock's voice broke her reverie. She only had her small rucksack to carry, and she swung one shoulder strap over her arm. She had done the right thing about John, hadn't she?

But there was no time to ponder. Adam Maclean came out of the lean-to when he saw them coming

and he greeted Sam with all the dignity befitting a
Chief's son. Lucy was surprised, but didn't show it.
Instead she asked Jock where she could wash, and
he led her along a pathway that wound through the
trees behind Adam Maclean's tent.

'The river cuts in through here,' he said, surprising her with the gentle flow of reasonably clear
water. 'Don't grind around in the mud. Lord knows
what'll be lurking down there. But apart from that
it's quite safe.' He caught her eye and grinned.
'Yeah, well, except for that lot. I'll go back and see
none of them wanders down here.'

She wanted to say, 'Make sure that includes
Adam Maclean,' but something stopped her. It was
as if she knew Jock would be shocked at the idea of
such ungentlemanly behaviour from their leader.
Gentleman! That was a laugh. And as she stripped off
and quickly slid into the water, it was disconcerting
to find herself contemplating exactly what Adam
Maclean was.

Why the preoccupation? Why was she bothered?
Lucy dived and felt the cool, delicious water rinsing
all the heat and grime from her hair. Then she surfaced and floated on her back, watching huge,
brightly coloured butterflies performing an aerial
ballet above her head. Life was chattering and
bustling around and above her. In the dense green
jungle the last of the day creatures would soon be
giving way to the first of the night. She thought of
crocodiles and shivered. Maybe she had been in
long enough, and swimming strongly towards the
bank, she climbed out and reached for her towel.
She gave it a shake before wrapping it around her-

self and perching down on a log that at one time must have come crashing down from the tangle between her and the sky.

There was no rush now, silly to worry about crocs, and she found her brush and slowly began untangling her hair. The butterflies had gone, frightened away by a parrot which had screeched out of a tree. Wasn't nature lovely ... Lucy fell into a dreamy, contemplative mood. She could still make out the vivid red flowers high up in the twisted festoons intertwining the trees. Long, Tarzan-like creepers hung from a high, dark canopy above. Why couldn't the world be left in peace, why did everything have to change?'

She glanced down at something on her toe. It was an ant—*ants*—oh no! But it was too late, they were everywhere, biting like red-hot needles, and she *hated* them. She was on her feet, stamping, screeching, trying to hit them off her. They were on the towel, *inside* it! She flung the wretched thing to the ground and started slapping her bottom and thighs. The little devils, they really hurt, and she stamped and kicked and slapped at herself for what seemed like ages.

'What the hell's going on? Good God!' Adam Maclean came pounding down the path and was suddenly rooted to the spot. Lucy was beside herself now, almost hysterical. She had to stop them, get them off her—and now *him*—oh no! She could have died with shame.

He came to, and before she could stop him he had bundled her into his arms—and had thrown her into the river! The fiend—the absolute *fiend*! But it had

worked. As she surfaced she realised all the ants had
been washed away.

'Better?' It was practically dark now, but by the
way he stood there, hands on hips, head on one side,
she knew he was laughing at her.

'I suppose you think that was funny!' she grated
through tight, angry lips.

'Not funny,' his voice shook, 'more like hilarious.'
Then he unbuttoned his shirt and held it out to her.
'Come on,' he said slowly, his voice a low, pulsating
thread. 'You can't stay in there all night. You'd
better come out and get dressed!'

CHAPTER TWO

'I'M not coming out until you go away!' Lucy floundered in the shallow water; it was difficult keeping her shoulders beneath the water without touching the bottom with her feet.

'Please yourself.' His voice was normally brusque again, almost as if this was all tiresome nonsense. 'But if I go I take my shirt with me.'

She kicked out as something nosed her foot. 'It doesn't matter—I've got my own clothes over there.'

'They're covered in ants—they're in your rucksack too. Whatever possessed you to put everything on the ground?'

'I didn't—they must have fallen off the log. You could hang it over there—your shirt—you could keep it off the ground quite easily.'

'But I'm already doing that.' He spoke with exaggerated patience, but she could tell that his lips were twisting into a taunting smile.

'The least you could do is turn round.' Her voice shook, but she quickly controlled it. He really was the most infuriating wretch she had ever met! Her eyes darted everywhere, looking for a means of escape. But undergrowth tangled down beside the bank, this was the only part that had been cleared.

'Maybe I don't want to turn round,' he went on,

coming even nearer to the edge and squatting down, all the more easily to see her, she guessed.

Suppose she could pull him in! Pretend to be asking for a hand out, and then when he was off balance she could give him a jank. That would show him. How *dared* he try to make a fool of her!

She swam closer. 'It's—it's a bit steep.' And her heart skipped about all over the place as she stretched out a hand. Strong fingers wound round hers, and as he stood up she braced herself against the bank, muttered a little prayer—then pulled.

But he was waiting for it. It was as if he knew what she had intended, and suddenly Lucy was being hauled, wet and protesting, into the fierce grip of two powerful arms.

'You little witch, pull me in, would you?' He pulled her against him, not caring, not even noticing, that she was soaking his bare chest and making long, damp marks on his trousers. Life seemed to be hammering away inside him; it burned from savage eyes and got tangled up in his breath.

'You devil—let me go!' Lucy squirmed and wriggled, but it only seemed to excite him all the more. Relentless hands swept possessively over her shapely, bare curves, and his face seared with wicked delight at each new discovery.

'That's no way to treat your rescuer.' His voice was alive with cruel mockery. 'You must know that it isn't every day that I get the chance to pull such a bewitching nymph out of the river.' He was gaining control now, his voice firm and level. There was no shame in his eyes, only a wealth of experience and more than a hint of the connoisseur. 'Come on,' he purred, 'be a good girl—give me a kiss.'

Lucy went hot all over and her knees suddenly felt weak. If he had let her go right then she would have collapsed in a heap. Then her strength returned in a blinding flash of hate.

'I'm not in the habit of kissing such world-weary bores!' she announced grandly, and that worked—that got him. He received the shock like a slap across the face.

His punishment was swift and effective. He kissed her—hard, long and very, very brutally. Her knees finally buckled, her senses swam, and the thundering power of his heart was easily matched by her own.

Then he almost threw her from him, but she stumbled so he caught her again. It was practically dark, but her slim young body was perfectly visible as a soft grey image, shapely and inviting.

'Whatever made me imagine I was holding a woman in my arms?' he ground out brutally. 'Packaging can be deceptive.' At long last he tossed his shirt at her. Her reaction certainly seemed to have surprised him. She guessed rejection didn't come often to Adam Maclean.

'The world doesn't begin and end with you, Mr Maclean.' She was decent at last, but it was a bit difficult doing up the buttons with trembling fingers. 'I may not have seen a white man for three months, but I've seen plenty of wild animals. And that's all you are—I know your type.'

'And you'll know me a whole lot better before very long, I promise you,' he warned, and he looked so big and strong, so dynamic and powerful, that Lucy almost faded away on the spot. Her heart began beating a loud and heavy tattoo, but she mustn't give in to this awful, soul-destroying fear.

With all the commotion they hadn't heard urgent footsteps treading lightly along the path. Nothing moved beneath the feet, no leaves rustled; the thick vegetation allowed the intruder to pass undetected.

It was Adam Maclean who was aware of him first, and they both spun round, suddenly aware of someone. It was Sam, almost indistinguishable in the gloom. Lucy had been a long time away from camp, he was obviously worried, but at the sight of the two of them he had stopped, and she saw a flash of bright teeth as he began to smile. Sam had always been enquiring about 'her man'. Now he would believe he had discovered the truth; and, satisfied, the young Indian boy stealthily dissolved back into the night as if he had been a ghost.

Lucy stared at the empty path, then up at Adam Maclean, and for maybe a minute they gazed at each other, a curious cord resting around both of them. They didn't speak, didn't move; it was almost as if he was trying to search her soul. But then the spell was broken, and the cold horror of realisation finally dawned.

What in heaven's name was she doing standing here? She was practically naked, had been naked a few moments ago. And with a man she had never met before—a total stranger.

Lucy wasn't the only one to recover her senses. Adam Maclean pushed her from him and gruffly commanded her to get properly dressed. So she tried buttoning his shirt again while he turned his back and gingerly picked through her clothes.

'You'd better go back to the tent,' he said, with crisp and perfect diction. 'Wait in there while I get these things sorted out under a light. Go along,' he said briskly, turning back towards her when he considered it safe. 'You'd better put some cream on those bites.'

Lucy didn't know how she staggered back to his tent. At least the canvas flaps had been dropped all round, and someone had hung up a lamp. A moth, a fairly small moth for these parts, fluttered about near the light, but for once she hardly took any notice of it. She felt jittery and jumpy. What had he done to her? What had happened?

She pulled herself together with an effort as pain made her peer down at her feet and legs. They were already quite pink and blotchy. And how was she supposed to put cream on them? Her first-aid kit was in the rucksack, and Adam Maclean still had that.

She heard him march past the tent, but he didn't stop, didn't *think* of bringing back her things. She peered round, but there was nothing except books and maps, and the radio of course. She suppressed a sudden giggle. Should she radio for help? Shout rape? Murder? That would get his fine expedition into plenty of trouble!

And there was still all that business to sort out. How could she stop him? Surely he must have some weak point in his plans. Whose help could she enlist? Was it possible to contact Felipe, who was attending a conference in São Marcos?

She heard him coming back, and moved quickly away from the radio to save him becoming suspicious. He pulled back the canvas and simply marched in.

'Here are your clothes.' He flung her jeans and a

clean check blouse on to a chair. 'And here's some cream for those bites,' he added, tossing a tube of something on to the table.

'I'll have my own cream, if you don't mind,' she told him calmly.

'Use *that*—get dressed—and don't argue!' She opened her mouth to protest, but he effectively stopped her by barking, 'The rest of your equipment is still being debugged. You've caused enough commotion for one evening. Supper is in ten minutes—make sure you're ready when I come back!'

'You can keep your rotten supper!' So silly, but it was the only thing she could think of to say.

He swung back on his tracks. 'I will not have this . . .'

'Insubordination?' she finished for him.

'*Childishness*, I was about to say.' Then he snatched up the tube of cream, and went on fiercely, 'Are you going to see to those bites—or am I?'

Fear calmed her. He would too—he really would have the nerve. 'I'll do it,' she muttered sulkily.

'Have you been bitten anywhere else—or just your legs?' he asked shrewdly.

'Nowhere I can't reach,' she said quickly, taking the tube before he changed his mind.

He frowned, his dark brows welding together, the lamp behind his head making a strange halo of his hair.

'Do what you please, only don't take any chances.' His eyes extracted her reluctant promise.

It was a bit difficult. Her bottom had been bitten in several places—the little devils! But it was her own fault. Fancy sitting on a log! Fancy staying out there alone in the gathering darkness! She dabbed away at herself and wondered how it would be when she put on some clothes. And she mustn't scratch them because they would turn nasty and probably leave a scar.

In the middle of the operation Adam Maclean came back. Lucy pulled the shirt down, but he didn't come in, just dumped her gear outside and went away again. She dressed quickly, the bites didn't feel too bad yet, then rummaged through her rucksack for her brush and perfume. Make-up was hopeless in the jungle, but she always made an effort to smell nice. Perfume was a good morale booster, so she applied a liberal dose.

Then, slowly, she began brushing her hair. It would be lovely to have something to eat, and it did smell quite delicious. She began to have visions of exotic food—ice-cream . . .

'We're ready.' Adam Maclean had just barged in again, and Lucy dropped the brush in surprise. 'They've gone to a lot of trouble,' he said quietly, 'so I won't stand for any nonsense. Understand?' Then he stepped aside and held back the canvas, saying in a loud, clear voice, 'After you, Miss Blake, if you please.'

Lucy was knocked out. Such *grace*—such charming manners. The man ought to have been on the stage!

Although the light had been quite dim in the tent, once outside, Lucy was momentarily blinded by the complete blackness of the jungle.

'Where's Sam?' she asked suspiciously, as Adam

Maclean took her arm and led her towards the
table.

'He didn't want to join us.' His deep voice floated
above her head, and the touch of his fingers above her
bare elbow seemed to bring her whole body alive.

She broke away and stumbled towards the fire.
But Adam Maclean had been right, Sam was
squatting beside the glow, happily preparing the fish
he had caught earlier. Satisfied, Lucy finally went to
join the others.

And they really had gone to a lot of trouble.
Planks had been propped up on oil drums to make a
table of banqueting proportions. It even had a cloth
that looked suspiciously like an old parachute which
had probably been used for dropping supplies.
There was a bowl of red, lily-type flowers she had
seen growing near the river, and those of the men
who didn't have beards had shaved.

Even Adam Maclean. She had been aware of a
faint spicy tang when he had come to the tent. And
he had changed as well; light grey slacks and
smooth, dove-coloured shirt. She felt conscious of
her old jeans and everyday check shirt. But then it
was a very different life to live out in the jungle
more or less permanently. She didn't have Maclean's resources, she didn't have the manpower or
the equipment to carry anything but the bare es-
sentials.

He pulled out a chair for her at one end of the
table. His breath caught her ear as he adjusted the
chair in place and she flinched and felt him draw
back quickly. With any luck her perfume would
have blown his mind.

Everyone finally sat down. Everyone, that was, except Jock, who now appeared from the cooking quarters they had camouflaged behind a truck.

'I'm afraid the first course is off this evening, madam,' he informed Lucy with regret, and while she pretended to look shocked, he placed before her a steaming, fragrant plate of what looked unbelievably like barbecued chicken.

Such unexpected, extravagant expedition food should have shocked her, but Lucy forgot all her good intentions and high morals, and polished off the lot as quickly and enthusiastically as any of the others. There was even some wine, in mugs and a bit warm, but it didn't matter. And it didn't matter about her old jeans and shirt, and before long she was laughing and flirting with them all. All except Adam Maclean, of course. He was stern and aloof, sitting far away down the table on the edge of darkness. As his men vied for her attention he watched them with a fixed, hooded expression. He didn't join in the fun, either. But by the end of the main course Lucy was past caring.

If these men hadn't seen a girl for nearly three months, then neither had she been in the company of such ineligible men. They were rogues really, she was quite sure of that. But there was safety in numbers, and her eyes sparkled and beamed in lively encouragement.

Two of them were scientists, jokingly referred to as 'the bird and bug men', who told Lucy they would be remaining at this camp to complete their experiments, which made some sort of base between civilisation and the advance party who had already struggled forward another fifteen miles.

As someone cleared the table, Lucy wondered why Adam Maclean wasn't charging ahead up front. She glanced at him, still sitting at the head of the table. Why did she get the feeling that he didn't belong here? When she had first heard of his expedition, when the radio message had come over the air from Kantara Park, they had told her that Adam Maclean was the expedition leader. When a leader wasn't up front and in the thick of it, he was back behind the lines, organising, trouble-shooting, chasing publicity and the ever-evasive financial aid. Expedition leaders didn't have a cosy little existence lazing away in the scientists' camp.

Lucy didn't have time to ponder. Jock produced a pile of plates and a large, lethal-looking carving knife, and put them down in front of her. The second course was about to be served and it looked as if they expected her to be 'Mum'.

It wasn't possible, it really wasn't. Lucy thought she must be hallucinating. Maybe those ant bites had poisoned her bloodstream. . . .

It was a cake—a large *chocolate* cake. Lucy's eyes widened, she had to shut her mouth before a moth flew in. Everyone laughed, even Adam Maclean looked slightly less fierce.

'I don't believe it. If only you knew how I'd *dreamed* of chocolate cake!' It was true; chocolate cake, roast beef and Yorkshire pudding. . . . 'You couldn't have made it out here, surely?' She was almost afraid to touch it with the knife in case it disappeared.

'Special delivery,' said Jock, nodding towards

Adam Maclean. 'Nearest to the comforts of home we're likely to see for a long time,' he added with a laugh, and there were rueful mutters of agreement all round.

Lucy managed to cut it up into eight, and while she did so, Adam Maclean spoke for the first time.

'I brought it with me,' he explained, 'along with the machine spares and more mundane items of food.'

'Like tinned chicken?' she answered quickly. 'I don't call that mundane.'

There was a sudden oasis of silence as far as the lamplight beamed. Beyond it the night was alive with screeches and incessant jungle calls.

'The chicken was for somebody's birthday—next week.' His expression said, 'Now argue with that'. Tension crackled between them, even the jungle seemed momentarily to hold its breath. Then the chatter broke out again, the rest of the wine was passed round. Lucy wondered if that had been for the birthday treat as well. Whose birthday? Just in case it was Adam Maclean's, she decided not to ask.

There was one slice of cake left, and as they refused to let her help with the clearing away, she wrapped it up in a paper napkin and went down to the river to find Sam. She knew he had a sweet tooth and the chocolate sponge was accepted with a delighted grin. He had slung his hammock fairly near the water's edge; she guessed he wanted to keep an eye on their boat. It wouldn't have surprised her if he even stayed awake all night.

He asked how long they were going to stay.

Lucy shrugged. 'I must still speak with Senhor

Maclean,' she said, in her limited Portuguese.

Sam laughed, his thick straight fringe swinging against the dark olive skin, then he made a joke in his own language. Lucy didn't understand, so he linked his fingers and mimed a huge stomach, indicating quite clearly that he soon expected her to be what he would call heavy with child.

Lucy tried not to look shocked. That would be fatal and he would go on about it for weeks. So she managed to pull a 'maybe, maybe not' kind of face and thanked heaven that there was nobody about to see. She placed a friendly hand on Sam's shoulder. How nice to be so straightforward, to be able to take things on face value. It just went to prove what an uncomplicated existence the Brazilian Indians led. Until the twentieth century had marched so ruthlessly into their lives. There was so much to be lost, so much that had already been lost. Measles and 'flu epidemics had wiped out dozens of tribes. And it would just go on and on unless something was done about it. A National Park wasn't the whole answer. There had to be a stop on progress—and a longer time of adjustment.

There was a movement behind them and they both turned to see Adam Maclean standing near. Cigar smoke clung to the humid air. How long had he been there? Had he heard them talking? Had he seen Sam's extremely obvious gesture?

He walked over and took the long cigar out of his mouth.

'I want to talk to you,' he said simply, and his tone suggested that there wasn't going to be a compromise.

'And I want to talk to you,' said Lucy, scrabbling to her feet and wishing Sam a pseudo-cheery good-night. Then she followed Adam Maclean a little farther down river, where the expedition boat had been tied up alongside. It was long and low, with a small cabin for'ard and a canvas awning hanging between poles over a large back deck.

Adam Maclean jumped aboard and when the rocking settled, he turned round and held out his hand.

'This is the only place where we're likely to have any privacy,' he said impatiently, when he saw her hesitate. 'I'm not likely to commit murder with your very good friend sitting just over there.'

He had a point, and Lucy allowed herself to be helped aboard. She jumped and landed awkwardly, so he had to steady her, and the brief contact of such a powerful body made her senses swim. She was obviously still a bit hazy from the wine!

'Mind you don't burn yourself.' He held his cigar out of the way, and she stumbled back, waiting under the awning while he went into the cabin and fetched a light. Sam's fire still glowed on the bank behind her and everything was suddenly heat and colour, darkness and confusion, strange contrasts that mingled with her emotions. The jungle pressed in on her from all sides, something long and evil snaked through the dark, fast flowing river. She felt sticky and hot and her heart seemed to be beating loudly in her ears. What was the matter? Why should she feel so odd just because Adam Maclean had touched her?

He came back outside, holding the lamp up high.

Lucy pulled herself together, although she had to squint for a moment against the light. Light and dark, beauty and danger. The jungle was a tangle of contrasts, it was sometimes difficult to leap from one of them to the other.

Adam Maclean fixed the light on a hook, then he leant against the high stern deck and propped one foot up on the engine box.

Lucy watched as he drew slowly and deeply on his cigar. If he was aware of her scrutiny he chose not to show it, as he contemplated the lazy coils of smoke without a care. Reluctant eyes flicked up and down the long length of him. His careless attitude accentuated the straining, lethal strength of his thighs. There was no hint of slackness around his waist, the stomach was hard and firm and the soft grey shirt spread upwards and outwards covering a powerful, bronzed torso that only a couple of hours before had felt virile and throbbing with the terrible urgency of his ruthless kiss.

Fear twisted inside at the memory. Was he remembering as well? Was he deliberately continuing the torture? Her eyes rose upwards, to find him steadily contemplating her as well.

The shadow of a moth danced across the pale halo of her hair; the blonde curls bounced down near her shoulders, framing a delicate oval face and beautiful eyes. Months of hard living had toned her body to a physical prime, her waist was trim and all her curves supple yet firm. The check shirt was a relic from schoolgirl days, and it strained a little between the buttons, tantalising aspect for a sexually dominant male.

Adam Maclean ground out his cigar and moved out of the light. 'I want to talk to you,' he began, his voice sounding tight and rigid, 'because I want to make it quite clear that you must leave here first thing in the morning.' Before Lucy could think of protesting, he went on arrogantly, 'Your behaviour this evening leaves me with no alternative. I shall expect you and the Indian . . .'

'Just a minute,' Lucy interrupted. 'What do you mean—*my* behaviour?'

He snorted. 'That shameless display at supper. I don't want someone like you causing trouble among my men.'

Shameless. Someone like me. If Lucy hadn't been sitting down she would have fallen over. 'After *your* behaviour down at the river, you *dare* to criticise me?' The cheek of him—the nerve!

'It's precisely because of that incident that I have no intention of leaving you alone.'

'Alone! What do you mean—alone? Surely if I'm by myself there'll be no one there to—to seduce.'

'You're being deliberately obtuse.'

'You could have fooled me. It's you who aren't making any sense.'

He sighed impatiently. 'I shall be leaving here soon after dawn. There could be trouble. Several of them are attracted to you. It isn't as if you're one of the team, someone they've come to know. You've just walked in on them—and they were totally unprepared.' Some battle seemed to be smouldering inside him. 'That's why I say that you have to leave when I do. You shouldn't be here anyway. I told you earlier—go back to the village; prepare the tribe to move south—soon—before the rains come.'

Lucy's mind was running ahead on wheels. She was scarcely conscious of what else he was saying. 'Where are you going?' she muttered carefully.

'Back to São Marcos.' He had said it before he could stop himself.

Her eyes lit up. 'Can I come with you?'

'Absolutely not.'

'But why?' A new note of pleading had crept into her tone. This was just the chance she needed. What hope had she of stopping this expedition if there was only her and Sam? But back in town, where she could contact friends, get in touch with the press. Maybe *then* she could find some way to beat him.

But Adam Maclean was nobody's fool.

'I'm not taking you with me for two very good reasons,' he began deliberately. 'One—I've got a shrewd suspicion that you'd only get in my way— start making trouble. . . .' She disclaimed any such idea, but he wasn't impressed. 'And secondly . . .'

'Go on—you can't stop now. What else do you suspect me of? Subversion?'

He hesitated a little longer, then finally stepped back into the light.

'Secondly,' he repeated, staring into her eyes. 'It could be a long trip. Two or three days. Two or three *nights*—here, together, alone on this boat.' She tossed her head in a vague inconsequential way, but he caught her chin and bent down to her level, and the whole kaleidoscope of excitement and fear started beating inside her again. 'Don't you know how you get under my skin?' he breathed crookedly. 'I couldn't trust myself, Lucy.' His fingers forced her to look up at him again. 'I couldn't trust myself,' he repeated ruthlessly, 'and after what I've seen during supper, I'm not sure if I could trust you.'

Lucy had never been so insulted in her life. 'What are you afraid of—that I might bite?'

Sensuality twisted his face and ran, strong and trembling, through his fingers. 'You're very lovely, you must know that. And you have a beautiful, provocative, extremely tempting body.' She tried to squirm out of his grasp, but he wouldn't allow it. There was no escape from his savage words as he grated, 'But you're not my type, my dear Lucy. Do you understand? I don't get my excitement from sleeping with young, inexperienced virgins—and I have no intention of starting with you.'

Virgin, was it? How did he know? 'I suppose you'd just *hate* yourself in the morning.' Somehow the words tumbled from the crazy jumble in her head.

He had turned away, proud and tense, but now he swung back and stared down at her from his great height.

'Such a remark,' he growled, 'only goes to prove how young you are. How young, inexperienced— and extremely foolish.'

CHAPTER THREE

LUCY lay awake that night long after the rest of the camp had settled down. With her hands folded behind her head, she stared up through the misty haze of mosquito net. Her body rocked the hammock slowly back and forth, but it didn't lull her to sleep. She couldn't sleep. She didn't have the time, because before dawn she had to come up with a plan that would stop Adam Maclean in his tracks.

But how? That was the problem. What about sabotage? But equipment could be replaced, even if she knew how to pull something vital off an engine—which she didn't. But they would be used to vehicles going out of service; it might delay them—but they wouldn't be permanently stopped.

She sighed, and rocked some more, knowing that whatever the cost, she wasn't going to let Adam Maclean run roughshod over her ideals. If she couldn't physically stop him, then the orders would have to come from high up. The only thing she could do was to get back to São Marcos. The Indian People's Fund would be very interested to hear that Maclean was planning to cut the Tukama territory in two. And if he was travelling back tomorrow, then she had to go with him—whether he liked it or not.

Only it wasn't as simple as that; in fact, it wasn't

really simple at all. First she had to persuade him to take her—and second ... Lucy hesitated, almost afraid to contemplate that other problem. The real problem was Adam Maclean, travelling with him—alone. When danger threatened she always got a strange tingling sensation up her spine. Just like the one that was tingling away now, the one that warned her that Adam Maclean wasn't a man to make idle threats. Inexperienced virgin, indeed! It galled Lucy to be regarded as nothing more than a silly child. She was a mature, passionate, extremely responsive young woman. How dared he make her sound so insipid and uninteresting! Not that she wanted to interest Adam Maclean, of course. The comparison was purely rhetorical.

She could picture him now, staring down at her under the boat's faded canopy. How tall, proud and terrifying, he had looked; yet so physically potent—so lethal and *male*.

She got the jitters just thinking about it all—yet strangely, every moment they had met seemed to be etched clearly in her mind. The way he had thrown her into the water, and how the getting-out process had got terribly out of hand. She had actually been standing there with nothing on—being kissed. She went hot again, feeling those strong, firm hands in their intimate caress. Why hadn't she screamed, shouted rape? Why? Because he fascinated her; it had to be admitted. She might hate him—and if anyone deserved being hated it was Adam Maclean—yet he had some incredible inner force that seemed to latch itself to her, and drain her senses dry. If she travelled back with him on his boat she

would be in more than one kind of danger. A man
like that could take so much—leave a girl shattered,
broken. Only she wouldn't! Not on your life. She
knew all about men and their one-track minds.
Adam Maclean didn't like rejection—and that was
all he would get from her.

The hammock was swinging quite violently now.
Lucy held her wrist in front of her face and gazed at
her watch's luminous dial. One o'clock. Was that
all? Her body wriggled with uneasy emotion. It
would be a good thing to forget all about the disturbing man sleeping not very far away in his hammock. She must concentrate all her attentions on the
job in hand. How was she going to persuade Adam
Maclean to take her back to town?

Why try to persuade him, a silent voice answered
back. Couldn't she smuggle herself aboard—stow-
away? But what about Sam? What about the hue and
cry when she was discovered missing? It wouldn't
take Maclean long to search his boat—and then
slowly, very slowly, her idea began to jell.

It was simple, so simple it just had to work. It
would mean leaving behind her hammock and mosquito net, she could never get them unhitched without rousing the camp. But apart from that there was
only her rucksack hanging in Adam Maclean's lean-
to. She would manage to tiptoe past him, collect her
bits and pieces, then go down to the river and wake
Sam.

Naturally, it was Adam Maclean who had to
wake up. Maybe she had landed a bit heavily on the
ground, and as she passed his hammock a low voice
muttered:

'Where do you think you're going?'

'Where do you think?' she snapped, cursing under her breath, and then having to go thrashing around in the undergrowth, just for appearances' sake. If there was a snake she would scream. If one dropped on her from a tree and bit, she would probably die, and it would all be Maclean's fault. But there weren't—and one didn't—so she made it safely back to the clearing and had to climb back into bed.

'Can you manage?' the same voice muttered in the darkness.

'Of course I can manage,' she puffed, because getting into a hammock wasn't easy, and a mosquito had just bitten her. Lucy felt very cross!

How long before Adam Maclean went back to sleep? She gave him an hour, then tried again. But she couldn't risk passing his way, the rucksack would have to stay behind. Damn!

All went well. Sam was awake even before she touched his shoulder. And he knew it was her. A grin was already spreading; no surprise, no distrust at such strange goings-on in the middle of the night.

'You must go back home—now,' Lucy whispered, struggling with her Portuguese. He looked puzzled, which was hardly surprising, and she held a finger to her lips and gestured that it would be dangerous to wake the sleeping man.

It took quite a bit of persuasion, but in the end he agreed. Tomorrow, she told him, she would be travelling to the city with Adam Maclean. Sam must return to his people, tell them where she had gone, that she would be coming back with a promise that there would be no new road. Sam still hadn't been sure, and she had been forced to prevaricate and suggest that Adam Maclean would insist that Sam came with them, and Sam and the big city wouldn't mix.

The young boy's only connection with civilisation had been the exaggerated horrors told when members of his tribe had returned from visits to the hospital. The stories weren't true—but now they served a useful purpose. Sam had no intention of delivering himself into the hands of the devil.

After that, Lucy had no further trouble, except to remind him not to start the boat's engine until he could no longer be heard.

His fire was out, his bits and pieces soon packed away. Lucy kept glancing anxiously towards the edge of the trees where the sleeping men lay. But there was no movement, and any sound Sam made was masked by the incessant cacophony of the jungle's night charade.

At last he was ready, and they rested a hand on each other's shoulder in a gesture of affection, before parting. Then Sam sprang nimbly into the bows, Lucy threw him the line, and he poled his way gently out into the current. He would make good progress downstream. He probably wouldn't go very far—not at night—but as long as he wasn't around in the morning, then Maclean would think that she had gone away with him. It was a pity about the rucksack, but it couldn't be helped. It would only be for a couple of days and she could make do with what she had on.

Now came the difficult bit. She had to climb aboard Adam Maclean's boat and find her way around. It wasn't easy.

At first she wondered if the cabin might be locked, but the door opened squeakily and she held her breath before slipping inside.

She groped her way around and hit up against a table-and-settee sort of arrangement, the type that slotted together to make a bed. But the boxed compartments beneath were too small to hide in. She was beginning to see more easily now. There was a two-burner stove and a sink, and a door forward. She investigated, but it was only the loo—no hope there. Surely there was somewhere. She came back into the cabin and peered round again. What about the hanging cupboard? But wouldn't Adam Maclean put his clothes in there? But the compartment next to it looked more likely, there were a couple of long macs already hanging there, some canvas, and a large plastic tub full of chain. Couldn't she hide behind that lot? If she piled everything in a heap, and covered herself with the macs. . . .

It took ten minutes of huffing and puffing, but finally Lucy was in, sitting on a pile of chain, covered by the canvas and macs. Only that was with the door still open, it would be dreadfully claustrophobic with it shut.

Her cell turned out to be a perfect torture chamber. It would have been so easy to have crawled out and snuggled up on the bunk. But supposing she didn't wake up in time? She could just imagine Adam Maclean's reaction if he found her lying there. So it was no good, she had to stay put. It was a long, chilly, damp and uncomfortable night, one Lucy knew she would never forget.

His voice woke her, she was amazed to discover that she had actually dozed.

'It's gone!' she heard Maclean shout back to the others. Then Jock said something, she couldn't hear what. She felt sick with apprehension—would her plan work or not?

'Seems strange,' Jock was saying. They were getting nearer now, probably on their way to check this boat.

Adam Maclean's voice was suitably gruff. 'Don't look upon it as a loss, Jock. Think of it as a gain.' Lucy fumed in the darkness. Cheek! How pleased he was to have got rid of her. The boat rocked as the two men climbed aboard and she closed her eyes and prayed.

'And what would I be doing with all that female equipment?' Jock was saying again. 'All that underwear, Snoopy tee-shirts and a bottle of fancy perfume?' Adam Maclean actually chuckled, and Jock went on, 'Do you want to take it—the rucksack—in case you meet some of her friends?'

Adam Maclean strolled very close to her cupboard. She could see him clearly through the louvred slats. He seemed about to say yes, but while Lucy crossed her fingers, he hesitated, and something made him seem to reassess.

'You'd better keep it—in case she—er—comes back.' Then they seemed to have gathered whatever they had come for, and the boat rocked again as they left.

Damn! Trust Adam Maclean not to listen to Jock. But her troubles still weren't over, she had to wait for Maclean to breakfast and load up the boat. It seemed a very long time before he finally stepped on board for the last time and started the engine.

Lucy's heart missed a beat as the throttle was opened and adjusted to meet the fast flowing current, as he pointed the boat upstream. They were off at last, and now all she had to do was wait here long enough for them to have travelled too far to turn back.

It was nearly midday when extreme thirst, an aching back and heat exhaustion finally forced her to break cover. Even Adam Maclean's fury would be preferably to another moment in that excruciating hell. Lucy pushed back the clutter and nearly fell out. The cabin door was open, through it she could just see Adam Maclean's elbow as he stood by the wheel.

It was now or never. He could either kill her or she could die of thirst. But it still took all her courage to gather herself upright and step out into the blistering heat. She held her breath and gazed up at him, but as she did so, he merely looked down at her and said,

'Hi! Fancy a beer?—there's some in the fridge!'

Lucy, quite literally, fell down. Her stiff, cramped knees buckled beneath her. Maclean dragged her upright and turned his attention back to the wheel.

'You mean you *knew*—all the time?' He paid no attention. 'Why didn't you turn back?' she croaked. 'Why did you let me stay in there? . . .'

He manoeuvred the boat around some floating debris, and when they were clear of it he turned round and gazed down at her with a supercilious grin.

'Work it out for yourself—I gave you fair warning. But if you're prepared to accept the consequences,' he shrugged, 'then why should I care?' His lips twisted into a dark, cruel smile. 'It's been a tough expedition—I could do with some light relief.'

'*I'm* not going to be your light relief,' she said crossly. If only her mouth wasn't so dry. What had he said about beer? And now she stumbled back through the cabin door and groped around for the fridge.

What bliss, what perfect luxury! Lucy found a cool can of lager and didn't even bother to find a glass. She gulped it down thirstily, washing away the hours she had spent in that dreadful place.

How long had Adam Maclean known she was there? And then she was suddenly so cross that she forgot all about caution and careered out on the deck again.

'Why didn't you fetch me out?' she said angrily, and when he looked nonplussed, she clutched her aching back and shouted. 'If you knew I was there all that time, why didn't you say so? I've been cooped up in there for hours!'

He remained irritatingly passive, brushing a fly off his shoulder and looking up at the sky as if expecting rain. 'I was just interested, that's all,' he said eventually. 'I wondered how long you'd be able to stick it. Hot, was it? I'm not surprised. Shouldn't think you got much air.'

Lucy went berserk. 'You mean to tell me that you let me stay in that hellhole just to satisfy some whim? How long was it? Huh? How long did you know I was there?' Her blonde curls quivered in fiery rage, but they didn't match the inferno inside her.

'I've no intention of telling you anything when you speak to me like that. You can calm down, young lady, and while you're about it, you can make yourself useful. Go and fix us some lunch, please, and fetch me a beer.'

Lucy boiled away inside, her eyes glued in fascination on his naked chest. 'Don't you "young lady" me!' she retorted, her mouth set in a mutinous line. He really was the most aggravating, infuriating man she had ever met! Why did he have to stand there looking so strong and unshakeable? Fancy being stuck with him for the next couple of days!

But he needn't think he was getting the better of her. He could whistle for his lunch. Lucy marched to the stern-deck and perched herself on it. There was some beer left in the can and she drained it dry.

For a moment nothing happened and she could watch her tormentor from a reasonably safe distance. The striped awning was giving them plenty of shade, which was probably why he had stripped off his shirt and changed long cotton slacks for a pair of minuscule shorts. He really did have incredible legs! Solid muscle power bulged beneath taut, bronzed skin. He was very athletically put together; broad shoulders and a powerful frame lightly balanced for immediate action.

The engine slowed and the gear shift was slipped into neutral. For an instant Lucy didn't realise what was happening until he left the wheel and she saw that the boat was simply drifting. She thought he was going to get something from one of the lockers under a seat. He moved slowly, lithely, until she looked up and their eyes met.

Anger shone from his face, which was alive and tense with emotion. Fear touched her, but it was too late. He grabbed a handful of her hair and pulled her head back; not really very hard, it didn't hurt much—except her pride.

'I *said* I wanted some lunch!' His other hand caught round her waist, and his fingers slipped under the blouse where it had pulled out of her jeans. 'I like my lunch about midday,' he said with a dangerous edge. 'Not mid-afternoon, or even tea-time. When I ask you to do something it has to be done then and there. Understand?' he finished quietly, and Lucy had the horrible feeling that she was about to be kissed.

'What did your last servant die of? If you want lunch, get your own!' Fine words—but they were a mistake.

He moved with the speed of a professional trained man. She was locked in a vicious grip, then bundled into the tiny cabin with her feet hardly touching the ground. His strength frightened her; the way he so easily manhandled her, his strong, hard body tangled up with her own. And there was pleasure and excitement in his eyes when he finally released her.

'If I have any more trouble I'll show you what happens when I'm *really* cross!' But he looked really cross right now. He looked like a man who saw what he wanted, whose need for a woman was as vital to him as the air he breathed. Anger and fury mixed with his passion and the battle was violent but shortlived. He breathed deeply, mastering his instinct, and the cabin seemed to hum and throb with the effort it cost him.

'I would like my lunch in ten minutes.' He spoke slowly; his voice still shook. 'Don't come out without it,' he warned fiercely, 'and *don't* be late.' Then he was gone, slamming the door behind him and heading straight back to the wheel. The gear was thrust into forward and the throttle opened into hard ahead. The boat responded and Lucy tottered on to a seat. Her mind tried to sort out a new twisting of threads. Her hands trembled and her knees felt incredibly weak. The life was knocked out of her, she had never been so physically drained by the absolute dominance of his body and mind. He was so strong, so resilient—but somewhere in the middle of it all he had roused her to excitement as well as fear.

Lucy staggered to her feet. Five of his ten minutes had already gone. If he wanted lunch, he could have it. But this was only round one, and Adam Maclean needn't think he had got the better of her yet. She would pay him back—make him realise just who he had dared to upset.

She thought they would have their lunch under way, but when she appeared on deck with the plates he was already nosing in towards the high, overhanging bank.

There was no question of climbing ashore, but he tied the bowline to a low trailing branch, then jumped down from the cabin roof and finally cut the engine. The noise didn't stop; it just changed from the relentless mechanical throbbing, to a throbbing of a live and vibrant kind. Parrots screeched out of the trees, bringing a flash of vivid colour from the mesh of dark, forbidding greens. What air there had been while moving was now still. They had stopped on a tight bend of the river which allowed no breath

of wind. Oppression hung in the steamy, uncomfortable heat.

The canvas awning shaded the whole cockpit
area, and Adam Maclean stretched out on one of
the seats which ran along the side, propping himself
against the cabin bulkhead. He didn't comment on
the strange assortment of lunch; slices of tinned
meat, some fruit salad, biscuits and cold baked
beans. That was how Lucy had pulled everything
out of the cupboard, although she had served it in a
more appropriate order.

She had only intended to pick at hers, but it had
suddenly seemed ages since their feast last night. She
had missed out on breakfast, and now her healthy
appetite couldn't be restrained.

But that didn't mean she had to indulge in cosy
conversation, so she resumed her perch on the stern
above the engine and pretended to watch out for the
parrots again.

Adam Maclean disappeared into the cabin, and
when he came back she heard the chink of glasses.
He had poured them both a long, cool, lemony
drink. He put it down beside her, just managing to
find enough shade. The awning didn't reach this far
back and the sun was already starting to burn her
nose.

'You shouldn't sit in the sun,' he said quietly, still
standing behind her, and to Lucy's astonishment he
dropped a sun-hat into her lap.

'It's mine. . . .' she began uncertainly, turning the
faded blue linen round and round in her hands.

'You didn't say please—so how about thank you?'
A new, husky note had crept in with the words and

as she struggled to put on the hat, her arm brushed against his bare chest. She peered anxiously under the brim and found him gazing down at her with an odd, mysterious look in his eyes.

Something stirred uneasily inside her. A tension was slowly building up and wrapping itself around them. She felt caught in a trap of insidious, sensual pleasure. For a second everything was more than real; the sun more dazzling, the day hotter, Adam Maclean's potent energy something exciting and dangerously male.

He sipped his drink, his eyes closing as his lips touched the glass, and long dark lashes curved against the taut, bronzed skin of his cheek. Thick, wayward curls flicked across his temple. Every plane of his face was so familiar now that Lucy dismissed the idea of having seen him somewhere before. Maybe she didn't know him—maybe she had just been expecting him all these years.

His glass was finally lowered, his eyes resting on it. But as she reached for her own drink she was aware that he was watching her.

'What are you doing here, Lucy?' he asked after a while, and when she gazed up at him again, he tapped her nose with an unexpectedly gentle finger. 'Was it a love affair gone wrong?' he almost whispered, and she swallowed and couldn't answer, and for once he didn't seem to mind. His hand touched her shoulder, and when she didn't object, he began tracing delicate circles across her back. Lucy bowed her head and let him follow the curve of her spine, up and down, up and down, in a slow, rhythmic pattern of utter delight.

All the stresses and strains of the past few months began to dissolve away. Alone in the jungle there had been no intimate human contact. No one to share her hopes and fears. No hand to hold, no shoulder to weep on.

Resistance drained from her like mountain rain. He sensed it and toppled off her hat, running his fingers through the blonde curls at the nape of her neck.

'My poor Lucy,' he murmured, allowing his lips to linger in her hair, then he raised her chin and planted an acre of little kisses all over her face. His mouth played over her own, the tip of his tongue found hers, it was only the merest hint of contact, yet it touched an intimate well of burning fire deep inside.

For just a moment it had been peaceful and calm, but as he raised his head and drew her inextricably into an embrace, she felt his body move with a restless, primeval stirring.

She was still perched on the stern-deck, her feet next to their glasses of lemony drink, her knees bent up because she had been leaning on them. Now she unfolded in a graceful coil, leaning back into his arms and letting him smooth the cottony jeans all the way up to her thighs.

'Were you very upset?' he whispered once more, and the eyes that searched hers seemed to see into the secret depths of her soul. 'Did he find someone else? Didn't he love you enough?' He pulled her shirt from the waistband, and as warm, strong fingers began undoing the buttons, his voice dropped to a low, husky throb as he murmured. 'Do you want me to show you how good love really is?'

Lucy had been hypnotised by the strange aura of his strength. But now she was suddenly panicked into action. She had heard all this before, over and over, and she wasn't that kind of girl—really.

'That just goes to show how wrong you can be,' she erupted, scrabbling down into the cockpit, tucking in her blouse and doing up the buttons with trembling fingers. 'You men are all the same— you're only after one thing. *Bed!* Is that all you can think about?' His expression of amazement had gone now, and he was just standing there, staring at her, looking tough and resilient, and daring to make a mockery of her love. 'Well, there's more to life than just sex, Mr Maclean.' He seemed to doubt it, but she battled on. 'And I've no intention of hopping into anyone's bed just to satisfy their ego. And anyway,' she went on, getting brave now and tossing her head, 'changed your tune, haven't you? I thought you said I wasn't your style—that you didn't go in for virgins. . . .'

'You've got to start some time, Lucy.' She gasped at the dreadful finality of his serious, thoughtful tone. Then his eyes ignited and little devils danced across his face, as he challenged. 'And I think you know perfectly well that you couldn't do any better than to begin with me!'

CHAPTER FOUR

'WHAT's the matter?' Adam growled, when she didn't reply. 'Scared? Frightened you might actually enjoy it?'

'You're disgusting!' Lucy marched into the cabin and slammed the door.

Why, oh, why did it always have to be like this? She had been so sure of John, sure that he truly did love her. And he hadn't always talked about bed—not to begin with. He was serious; the youngest tutor in the University. It was he who had first nurtured her interest in the South American Indians. She had been so sure that he had been interested in her as a person. And then it had begun; the 'you-would-go-to-bed-with-me-if-you-loved-me' bit. She did love him, but she didn't want to have to prove it. And it wasn't right. They hadn't even suggested marriage. John's loving persuasion had soon turned to frustrated anger. If she couldn't grow up he would find himself a real woman. Only he hadn't, he had wanted her, and the pressure continued until it became impossible to bear.

They had talked about coming to Brazil, and Lucy went ahead with her plans, contacting the Kantara National Park and arranging to continue with her research. It had been the right decision—it *had*. John would find someone more—amenable. Trouble was, the whole world was full of men—and here was another one with only one thought in his head.

The engine started and she heard Adam walk across the cabin roof to untie the line. Then he jumped back down beside the wheel, and they were off again. Lucy breathed more easily. He wouldn't be able to do anything when they were under way.

But that didn't stop them looking at each other. What was different about him? Why did she never think of John, or miss him, when Adam Maclean was near?

It was mid-afternoon and she had cleared up the lunch things just to keep out of the way. But it was too hot and stuffy in the little cabin, so she had stretched out on the slatted seats under the awning and pretended to go to sleep. But with her sun-hat tilted forward she had enough camouflage to carefully open her eyes. And in the hot, thick heat of the steamy afternoon, she looked long and hard at Adam Maclean and came to a few disturbing conclusions.

He was the most lethally attractive man she had ever seen. There was something about him, some inner pulsating life that reached out and kindled a fiery spark of her own. Virgins weren't his style. What was his style? And Lucy found herself actually contemplating what he would be like in bed! But before they got to bed, how would he undress his woman? A button undone here—a kiss there. Her imagination supplied its own twist of pleasure as she pictured lacy underwear slowly peeled off. She could almost feel his soft thick hair tickly against her skin. . . . But what then? . . . How would one of his experienced women behave?

Lucy tried to imagine being possessed. But wouldn't he want much, much more? How would you make love to someone who had seen it all— done it all? No wonder he found virgins a bit of a bore.

He suddenly took his hands off the wheel and stretched long, suntanned arms up above his head, as if he was stiff, or restless, from so much inaction. The strained muscles down his back accentuated the deep groove of his body line, and the tops of his thighs pressed together as he gave a long, shuddering sigh.

As he dropped his arms and relaxed, he turned round quickly, and she wasn't quick enough closing her eyes.

'I think it's time you took a turn at the wheel.' He stood aside and Lucy reluctantly dragged herself over. 'Shout if you don't like the look of anything.' His lips twisted curiously, and Lucy knew her appraisal had been discovered. 'The river's quite deep for a while, you shouldn't have any problem.'

At least with him out of the way Lucy was able to concentrate. She wasn't used to boats, but there wasn't much chance of meeting more than a native dug-out canoe coming the other way. Yet today it appeared that they were the only people using the dark ribbon of murky water. The current was very strong in parts and the throttle had to be opened up if they were to keep making headway. The scene didn't change, it went on and on, relentless and pervading; the dark green tangle of jungle pressed in from all sides, spilling over the bank into the water on occasions, and once she saw a group of crocodiles basking in the dry mud in a worn-out hollow. Lucy nearly called Adam. Supposing one of them slipped into the water? Could they sink the boat? But she didn't want to call him, didn't want him out here with her again, so she kept a wary eye on the evil monsters and crawled past them, cutting the motor as slow as she dared.

One of them yawned and she held her breath; the cabin door was flung open. 'What's the matter? Why have you slowed down . . . ?'

She hissed him to silence and he followed her gaze, turning back and laughing silently at her agitation.

'It's too hot for them to worry about us,' he said with irritating calm. 'You look hot yourself.' His eyes licked over her. 'Don't mind me—strip off if you want.'

Lucy wouldn't lower herself to reply, but as he climbed back through the cabin door, she opened the throttle hard and the boat leapt forward. Adam missed his footing and nearly fell.

'I'm most dreadfully sorry,' she drawled, with wide and innocent eyes. 'Can't get the hang of this stupid thing at all.'

He growled under his breath, probably something uncomplimentary. Lucy smiled to herself and settled down again at the wheel. Maybe this trip wouldn't be as bad as she had foreseen.

Her confidence swept them along for another couple of hours. Adam sat writing something in a leather-bound book. He was stretched out on the bench beside her; if she glanced down past her elbow she could just see his bare foot. Then he shifted and began peering out under the awning, astern.

Lucy pretended not to notice. There was a bit of a breeze now, which made a nice change and the current must have changed because it began to feel a bit rough.

'I'll take over.'

She shrugged. 'As you please.' But it had been a bit of a strain, and really she felt quite relieved. Then as she turned round she saw it. 'How long's that been there?' It was the biggest, blackest cloud she had seen since being out here.

When it rained in Brazil, it really did rain.

'Get inside!' Adam had managed to find a little nook of river-bank to nose into. It was a tiny bay, probably a watering hole, and they had to squeeze in under the trees and out of the turbulent current. He had scrabbled ashore and made them fast; and now, as he clambered back on board, with Lucy anxiously hanging over the rail, the heavens opened and it was like somebody turning on a huge tap.

Lucy had never been on a boat in a thunderstorm. It was as black as night until the lightning crackled and lit up even the darkest shadows. Adam made some tea. They couldn't speak; rain hammered on the cabin roof like machine-gun fire. And there were bangs and thumps as pods and things fell off the trees. Supposing one of the trees was hit by lightning? Supposing the boat was hit ... and with all this water. ... She glanced out of the cabin porthole. The river was beaten flat under the torrent, but debris shot past the boat at a terrific rate. The wind howled through the trees, she could see those on the far bank tossed and torn by the violence of the tropical storm. Lightning flashed again, a great crack of thunder preceded a loud, threatening rumble. Lucy jumped and hot tea spilled on to her leg. And all the time Adam sat there with his nose in the same wretched book.

'How long—how long do they usually last?' she attempted to ask above the racket.

He looked up at her, but his mind was a long way off. 'Can never tell. Maybe an hour—maybe more. . . .'

'That long?' It was difficult to try and sound casual.

His lips moved as he tried not to smile. 'There's nothing to worry about. Spectacular really. Why don't you strip off and go out on deck?' He held up a hand to stop the outburst. 'I didn't mean—I spoke without thinking.' But then his eyes roamed over her sensuous curves. 'Still, it might be a good idea. Fancing sharing a shower?'

Another great crack exploded overhead. Lucy gasped this time, she couldn't help it, and her hands began to shake.

'You're really scared, aren't you?' He offered his hand. 'Come on, sit over here. Tell me all about the Indian village, tell me all about Sam.'

She perched on the edge of the bunk, as far away from him as she could.

'You don't have to be polite,' she said in a tiny voice. 'I know you're not interested. You don't have to treat me like a child.'

His expression darkened. He had put his shirt

back on, the one with the buttons and tabs; it made
him look hard and military, and more attractive
than ever.

'I thought that's what you were,' he said sharply.
'I thought you wanted me to treat you like a child.'
Lightning seared through the heavy air, thunder
growled overhead again, Lucy went whiter than
ever and he relented. 'It's all right, nothing's going
to happen. Come here.'

This time when he reached out Lucy bolted into
his arms. She clung to him, stiff with terror. She had
always hated thunderstorms, even at home . . .
There was another thud on the roof, and he held her
tight, one large hand slowly stroking her hair.

It took a long time, but slowly, very slowly, all
her fear evaporated away. She could still hear the
crashing and banging and the torrential rain, but
the noise had drifted into the background. Instead,
she listened to the steady pounding of Adam's heart.
It felt so good to be next to him, as if she belonged.
As if it were natural for him to tame his savage
strength in the act of her protection. The next time
the thunder cracked she didn't even move.

Only for some reason he was suddenly cross.
'Careful,' he warned, with dark, troubled eyes, 'you
might actually start enjoying yourself.'

Unaccountably hurt, Lucy sidled along to the
other end of the bunk-settee. He couldn't be nice,
could he? Not even for five minutes. If only there
was some way she could get away!

She rubbed her arms, trying to rub the feel of him
away. 'Any enjoyment I might feel has got absolutely nothing to do with you.' She was quickly on

the defensive. Too quickly—and she tried to think of a way to take his mind off her vulnerability.

'How could I enjoy anything with you? You're nothing but a—a—jailor—a torturer!' Her eyes swung round the cabin. 'Making me stay cooped up in that cupboard for hours and hours. . . .'

'I don't remember inviting you on board.' His stern face was horribly grim. 'So you're not really in a position to complain.' He had to shout to be heard above the noise. They were both shouting. It was a good excuse to get a few home truths sorted out.

'How *did* you know I was there? Or were you just saying that—*pretending* you knew?'

'You may not be *dressed* much like a woman,' he growled, getting really cross because she wouldn't let him get on with his book, 'but that sure is some fancy perfume you've got on.'

'You mean you could smell it?' Her blue eyes opened wide.

'Isn't that the point?' He picked up his book again and turned the page.

'But when?' she persisted. 'You didn't come in here all the morning. Not once we'd left. . . .'

He sighed impatiently and pushed away his book. 'If you must know, it was earlier, when I came in here with Jock. I could hardly miss it. Bit pungent, isn't it, for the outdoor life? Or do you always go round smelling like a flower garden?'

Flower garden! It had cost a fortune. 'It was a present from John,' she said, without thinking.

He wasn't impressed. 'I like a woman to smell like a woman. Do you know what the French call it . . . ?'

Lucy ignored him. 'You mean you knew before we left—when Jock asked you to look after my rucksack?' And when he didn't deny it, but just sat there looking cool and smug, she thumped her fist on the table and made the tea mugs jump. 'Of all the lowdown, dirty, despicable things! My clothes are in there—things I need.'

'Tough!' His eyes returned her hate. 'But then I'm not really interested in your state of dress, am I? The only thing I care about is the successful completion of my expedition. I can do without your interference. You shouldn't be here, as you very well know. You should be back with the Tukama—not on some joyride with me.'

'Joyride! If you think being on this horrible boat with you is a joyride, then let me put you straight. This is the last place on earth that I want to be. If you were the last *man* on earth I wouldn't want to be anywhere near you.'

'Who says you'd get the chance?' he interrupted, with unholy glee.

'Oh . . . !' Lucy shook with frustration. Was there no getting through to the wretched man? 'You've got a one-track mind. I hate you, Adam Maclean! Do you hear?' she bellowed. 'I hate you and your kind!'

She really thought she had gone too far this time. It suddenly stopped raining, the silence was intense. Conflict and excitement beat a tattoo in the thick, heavy air. Adam's face was as black and fierce as the dark, thundery sky.

'Hate away, my little white virgin—hate away.' His eyes devoured her, like a hawk hovering about its prey. 'Hating's safe—but it's a waste, Lucy, a waste of your passion and mine. It's time you grew up—faced facts. We both know where this trip is leading us. You made your decision when you stowed away.' She tried to protest, but a warning hand silenced her. 'So pretend to dislike me all you please. But what's going to happen when I start to change your hate into desire?' His lips twisted in a sensual expression of expertise. 'Do you doubt that I could?—or that I would?' She fled and his cruel laughter ran beside her.

Could he? Would he? Everything was wet outside, so she had to patrol up and down, up and down, wringing her hands together. This was dreadful, she had never experienced anything like it. What was the matter with her? Was she only pretending to hate him? If so, what did that mean? She stared down at her shaking fingers and stuffed them out of sight in the pockets of her jeans.

What a mess! She did hate him—she did. Even if it hadn't been for this Indian business, Lucy knew she would have disliked him on sight. Was *that* his plan? She gasped at his audacity. Was he trying to soft-soap the opposition out of the way? Make her fall in love with him—so that by the time they reached São Marcos she would be eating out of the palm of his hand. Huh! And how long would that last?

Calmer now, she leant on the side rail and tried to tell herself the truth. She remembered those few crazy moments on the stern-deck at lunchtime. The momentary timelessness and peace. The feeling of fusion, deep and instinctive. Had that been nothing

more than the beginning of his plan? She closed her
eyes and felt again his lips on the nape of her neck.
The way her gently roused body had unfurled for
him. . . . Hot tears of humiliation smarted her eyes.
Yes, if she allowed it to happen, it would be very
easy to fall in love with Adam Maclean. But at least
now she knew. And she wouldn't get herself in that
sort of predicament again.

So how was she going to survive the next couple
of days?

Humour him? Impossible! The man was beyond
decent feeling. But she would have to try not to ag-
gravate him, even if she exploded in the attempt.
From now on it would be 'yes, sir—no, sir'. And
Lucy stayed outside contemplating her plan, hardly
noticing as the dark tropical night took over from
the heat and turmoil of the blistering day.

She didn't notice when the cabin light had come
on, and now there was a smell of cooking. Probably
some dehydrated stew in the process of being res-
urrected. Perhaps it was time she went on. Lucy took
a deep breath and tried to look something like
normal.

All went well during supper. He didn't look at
her—so she didn't look at him. She even offered to
wash up—so he made the coffee, and while they
drank it he switched on the radio receiver and listened to the evening call from the advance party
back to the scientific camp. Then someone else
began speaking, only the atmospherics were too bad
or the person too far away.

'That's the control house—back in São Marcos,'
Adam explained, switching off the set to conserve

the batteries. 'We can't pick them up on this. But they'll be asking if I got away on time.'

'Will they be sending the plane to come and get us?'

He nodded. 'The day after tomorrow. We'll have quite a walk from the river to the airstrip.'

Lucy wasn't in a position to moan—so she didn't. There was an awkward pause. Adam looked as if he wanted to say something, only he wasn't sure what.

'Who—who was it on the other end—back at control?' she asked, just for something to say.

'Don't know,' he shrugged, and there was suddenly no expression in his eyes. 'Could be Ken, that's the expedition doctor, or—one of the others.'

Lucy wasn't really bothered, but at least when he was preoccupied she felt safe. She yawned unexpectedly and tried to stifle it. She really was tired. A night in a cupboard hadn't helped. But there was the problem of sleeping tonight. Had Adam brought a hammock? Would the poles of the canvas awning take his weight?

At last he decided it was time to make a move. 'How are the bites?'

'Itchy!'

'Let me see.'

It was safer not to argue, so she slipped off her flip-flops and showed him her ankles and feet.

'What about the others?'

She stared at him woodenly. 'Much the same.'

He nodded. 'You're not scratching them, are you?'

She wanted to say, 'Does it look like it?' but said simply, 'No,' instead.

'You'd better put some more cream on them,'

and he fished out a tube from his medicine chest.

Lucy thought of her own supplies back in her rucksack. But she didn't mention them, even managed to keep the accusation out of her eyes. Then she asked if he had any malaria tablets. 'The sort you take every day.'

'These do?' He held out an identical pack. They could have been her own—but she didn't ask. They had got through the evening without arguing, but she still felt jumpy because there was still this question of bed.

She took the pill, then dived into the loo to anoint her blotches. There was a tiny basin, so she stripped off and managed to wash. If he didn't like her using his towel it was too bad. Then she rinsed out her underclothes, then realised that meant putting on her jeans and blouse again. Wretched man! She could visualise all her things still back at the camp. She hung her bra and pants over the hot water pipe. Keep calm—don't make a fuss.

There had been a few bangs and bumps from the main cabin while she had been occupied, and when she returned she soon saw why. The table and settee arrangement had been collapsed together, the backrest now formed the mattress and it made quite a sizeable double bed. A mosquito net had been draped over it. All mod. cons! And Adam had gone outside, as well. How thoughtful. She wondered if he was having much trouble with his hammock.

She heard his footsteps on the cabin roof. What was he doing up there? Should she get into bed, or wait for him to call out goodnight? Uncertainly, she peered out of the window in the cabin door. He was

standing looking out over the stern now, smoking a
cigar; she could see the dull red glow as he turned
his head.

Better wait. Lucy darted away from the window
and tried to make herself busy putting away his
book. She had idly flicked over a few pages, when
he came back in. His cigar had vanished, and he
made a great thing about not looking at her, as he
muttered:

'Which side is yours?'

For a moment she stared at him blankly, then
everything began to fall into place. 'The inside,' she
retorted sharply. 'In here. That's where you are—
out there.' It was beginning—trouble, just as she
had feared.

'Is that a fact?' He waggled his head in a stupid,
disbelieving manner. 'Well, I hate to disillusion you,
my dear Lucy, but after the kind of day I've had I
need a good night's sleep. There,' he pointed, just in
case she hadn't got the message.

'Suit yourself.' She could tell he was surprised
that she didn't argue. 'I realise you're not a gentleman, nor ever *said* you were,' she added, as he
began to speak. 'You sleep where you choose, Mr
Maclean. It's your boat—and it's your bunk. Sweet
dreams!' She swept up one of the blankets as she
passed out of the cabin door. It wasn't actually raining now, that was something.

'Don't be ridiculous, child.' He might think her
one now because it suited him. But in there, lying
next to him . . . ? No way!

'I shall be perfectly comfortable!' Lucy found she
was quite good at playing the martyr, but actually

she was shaking inside. The whole incident could turn explosive. She prayed for strength to keep the spark of ignition well out of the way.

'Lucy, if it rains again you'll get wet.' Oh, how sensible, how calm and reposed—Lucy wasn't the least impressed.

'The awning will keep me dry,' she reminded him coolly, settling down on the wooden seat and trying to look comfortable, but he simply swore under his breath and marched back into the cabin, slamming shut the door.

Was that all? Wasn't he going to try and persuade her some more? It was quite damp and chilly and Lucy wound the blanket round herself, but it was no good, and she sat up again.

Were there any creepy-crawlies about to fall on her? And what about those crocodiles? She peered over the side and watched bits and pieces floating by in the current. Then the cabin light went out and it was all screeching jungle noises and utter blackness.

Maybe it wasn't such a good idea to sleep so close to the sides. Did snakes climb up into boats? Lucy shivered and shuffled over to the middle of the floor. It was hard and uncomfortable, but it would probably be drier here, if it rained.

She didn't really expect to sleep, yet after a night spent in a cupboard she felt that she ought to drop off anywhere. She actually managed to doze once or twice, waking suddenly as something bumped against the boat. But nothing happened, perhaps it was a log washed down the river by the torrential storm.

She woke again when it was raining. Not as bad

as before, just a steady downpour. But there wasn't so much wind this time, and not a lot blew in from the sides. Good thing she had moved . . . .

It was later—how much later she didn't know. There was a new noise, something sharper—like a crack. It came again, from above, and more puzzled than afraid, Lucy peered up. There seemed to be a heavy bulge above her head. The old awning had collected a lot of water. There were a few rips in the canvas, she had noticed before, but there were no drips near her. Then the noise came again, and with it a sudden gust of wind. The old awning ripped; the flood poured down. Lucy was soaked to the skin.

'Oh no!' She shrieked with frustration. There was nothing else she could wear. And the blanket was wet through. She groped around, untangling herself from blanket and canvas, cursing Adam in the darkness. He knew this would happen, that was why he'd let her stay out here.

She heaved herself up and tugged some more. A whole lot of canvas fell on top of her; the cabin light flicked on, but it only made things look worse, and Adam was suddenly untangling a heap of very angry, very wet young girl.

He pulled her to her feet and surveyed the havoc. Then giving vent to anger as it welled up inside him, he roared, 'That's it—that does it. Get inside—quick!'

CHAPTER FIVE

ADAM hauled Lucy into the cabin, the door swinging dangerously on its hinges. She had never seen him, *anyone*, look quite so violently angry before. The close confinement throbbed with the intensity of his burning rage. 'Look at you,' he fumed, 'just look at the state you're in!'

Lucy didn't want to look; her blouse was plastered against her and was practically transparent. As her chest rose and fell in fury, Adam's menacing eyes gleamed.

'It wasn't my fault,' she shouted, all her good intentions cast to the wind. Had she really ever hoped to appeal to his better nature? Hah! What a waste of time that had been. 'It was *your* canopy that broke,' she went on fiercely. 'It's your rotten boat, not mine!'

'And who insisted on sleeping out there on a night like this?' he bellowed. 'You haven't got anything else to wear.'

'Whose fault's that?' Lucy rounded on him. 'I've got a rucksack full of gear back at your camp!'

He refused to acknowledge it. 'Where's your blanket?' he said instead.

'Outside!' Honestly, where else did he expect it to be?

'I suppose that's soaking wet too.'

She smiled a tight, gracious smile. 'Right first time.'

'What,' he asked distractedly, 'what on God's earth have I done to deserve you?'

'Deserve me! *You're* all right!' Lucy was working herself up into a fine old temper now. 'I'm the one who's soaked to the skin. I'm the one who's stranded without so much as a toothbrush or comb. That's what you've done, Mr Maclean. You knew I was on this boat, yet you refused to bring along my things. It's someone up there paying you back for such a despicable trick!'

'Witch, are you?' He twisted his hands into her wet, straggly hair. 'But don't be too sure your spells are going to work on me.' His face was close to hers, dark, menacing—Lucy could hardly breathe.

'I wouldn't waste my time casting them on you.' She twisted away from him, her slim, shapely figure accentuated by the wet fabric and low cabin light.

He tried to control himself, but the muscles down his neck strained with the effort. 'It's about time you started being thankful that you haven't ended up crocodile food. I can do without this aggravation. . . .'

'Then why didn't you haul me off the boat when you first knew I was here?'

'I wish to God I had!' Then he marched over to the wardrobe and pulled out a shirt. It was the one he had been wearing yesterday, the one he had handed to her down at the river. A quick flood of memory returned, but there was no resemblance between the taunting seduction as he had watched her swimming, and the pure violence of his anger now.

'Get into that,' he snapped, flinging the shirt at her, 'while I clear up the mess outside.'

Lucy knew she wouldn't have long, and while he clattered and banged about outside she took refuge in the loo again and peeled off. Her underwear hanging on the pipe was still wet. Damn! But at least the voluminous shirt respectably covered all moving parts! She had to roll the sleeves up, so that she could see her hands, and the top button was a long way down her cleavage—she would just have to keep out of the light!

When Adam came back, his dark, watchful eyes swept over her before darting away. She felt suddenly confused as he picked up a towel and started drying himself off. He was only wearing shorts, which had been bad enough during the day. But now, at night, the broad powerful torso and muscular legs riveted her attention. Lucy felt breathless and her heart began working overtime, as the towel was pulled briskly over such fascinating skin.

She dragged her eyes away and began fiddling with one of the buttons. He was still very angry, hardly in control of himself, his breathing seemed to be coming in rapid bursts.

He hung up the towel and his face was set with grim determination.

'Lucy,' he began, very, very carefully, 'we only have one blanket—and there's only one bed. There's nothing I can do about it—and we both need a good night's sleep. Now, do you intend getting in that bed before I get really upset?'

She could tell from his tone that it was already too late.

'I'm not going. . . .' But she got no further. He grabbed her by both shoulders and tossed her on to the bed.

She scrabbled up.

He pushed her down.

'Lie there. Keep quiet! And stop making such a fuss!' Strong arms pressed her into the mattress and she arched her back and squirmed and wriggled. But he wouldn't let her go as he began to look more and more like the devil. 'If you lie still I'll be able to get some sleep,' he growled, excitement and heat beating out of him. 'But if you thrash around— make me *really* angry, then there's no saying what I might do. Virgin or no virgin,' he added for good measure. He was breathing hard now, his face aflame with a cruel edge of delight. He seemed almost to be willing her to disobey, so that it would give him the excuse for rape.

Lucy gulped and went limp. It was the only possible thing to do. He wasn't joking; he really meant what he said. She closed her eyes and prayed that the flood would ebb.

When he was satisfied, he finally released his grip. Her arms hurt where his fingers had bruised the flesh, but she refused to let him know it. Instead she pressed herself hard against the cabin side so that she wouldn't have to touch him. She would lie here if she must—but that didn't mean she had to go to sleep. He rummaged around with the mosquito net and finally turned out the light. His body was tense and alive, waiting for her slightest movement. Lucy held her breath and kept her body rigid.

It was a long time before his breathing steadied and soon after that she could tell he was asleep. Now, at last, she finally relaxed and rolled on to her back, prepared to stare all night into the misty white protective curtain. Adam had turned from her, if she moved her eyes she could see the strong naked column of his back. Lucy tensed again, but not for long. Fear and exhaustion finally took their toll—and she, too, slept.

She was being crushed alive, unable to breathe, panicking—it was part of her dream a long time before she finally woke up.

Adam's great arm had been flung across her chest. He had rolled over on to his stomach. If she had turned her head her nose would have buried itself in his hair. How could he breathe like that? Come to that, how could she? Then he moved in his sleep and his arm slid down, resting comfortably above her waist.

Lucy relaxed again, until she realised he was touching bare skin. His wretched shirt had ridden up in the night. Lucy went hot all over. Then carefully, very carefully, she began to wriggle it into place.

Adam groaned and gave a couple of snuffles. He stretched, slowly and luxuriously, slipping momentarily into consciousness, then drifting back to sleep.

The shirt had to wait after that. She wouldn't risk disturbing him again. Except now his chin was digging painfully into her shoulder.

So she moved, just a little bit, and he wriggled closer. It was rather nice, actually; Lucy's cosy early morning haze was distorting her senses. But now his hair was tickling her nose, so she screwed up her face and tried to blow it away. He sighed sleepily and his thumb began caressing the smooth skin beneath her ribs.

Lucy held her breath, and he floated off again. Phew! But she couldn't rest now. How strange it felt to be lying half-naked with a man she could only call Maclean. Funny that! His name was Adam, but she wouldn't dream of calling him that.

Imagine going to bed with someone you weren't even on first name terms. Lucy's humour bubbled inside her, then, more seriously, she began practising his name. Not aloud, but in her mind's ear, whispering it softly, lingering it into a prayer. Adam—Ad-aaaam.

He stirred again, but this time Lucy didn't worry. He was practically asleep. So she closed her eyes and gave an experimental wriggle.

'Morning, darling,' he breathed huskily, somewhere near her ear.

Darling! Who did he think she was? Heavens. Maybe she should wake him up—but supposing he was cross. . . . Better keep still. Better to humour him. In a minute he would drop off to sleep.

But this time he didn't. He didn't wake up, exactly, just stretched and moaned and seemed to enjoy an intimate exploration of the curve of Lucy's hip.

His lips touched her cheek in the merest suggestion of a kiss, yet it wasn't her he was meant to be kissing. It was someone else, someone he quite obviously expected to wake up with. Half of her wanted to shout, 'It's me—it's *me*!' But the other half, the treacherous half, wanted to stay by his side and see what would happen. After all, she judged, he couldn't be *very* dangerous when he was so beautifully drowsy. . . . But that was a mistake only virgins could make!

It wasn't long before Lucy realised she had made a grave mistake. Adam slowly rolled her into his arms until they were lying there, facing each other, side by side. Did he always make love with his eyes closed? Why, thought Lucy, doesn't he know it's me?

'I didn't sleep very well,' he murmured softly, 'you kept disturbing me.' His eyes were still closed, he was still very sleepy. Lucy didn't dare to reply. She didn't want to spoil the peace of it all, and the warm glow that was slowly spreading inside. If she opened her eyes just a little, she could peer up and gaze into his face. She had never seen the stern lines look so utterly at ease. Yet, as he moved restlessly against her, she saw the skin stretch taut across his cheeks.

His gentle, caressing embrace melted her soul. In a minute it would stop, he would realise who she was, and she could always pretend to have been asleep. Then, with lingering ease, he searched out the warm invitation of her lips. He parted their sensuous softness with a tender yet assertive strength, and when she responded like an unfurling flower he gave a little moan of delight.

It was all a dream, an incredibly sensuous dream, as he coaxed and caressed reality away.

'You're so beautiful.' And his hands sent a perfect message to his brain. As he drew her closer she could feel the need for her rousing within him. No instinct warned her to stop him as he began unbuttoning her shirt, and Lucy gasped as their legs entwined and it was bare flesh next to bare flesh.

Desire suddenly flooded, hot and strong, through her veins. There was an aching void strangely full of longing. Was this what love meant? Was this what John had meant? With crashing realisation, Lucy knew she had never felt like this before. Now, as she clung to powerful, muscular shoulders, joy and excitement mingled with the agony and pain. That any man could do such wonderful things to her. . . . And it felt so naturally right—so real. . . .

She reached down and ran her fingers along the strong column of his neck. Then she spread her palm and smoothed a firm path across his back.

Adam shuddered and eased his way sleepily back to her lips. 'I want you badly,' he whispered, tormenting her with his long, hard, body in a slow, insidious rhythm. 'And I think you want me too. . . .'

And she did. Every little part of her burned to be possessed. She felt alive, a real woman for the first time in her life. And it didn't take experience, just instinct and love, to know exactly how to please him.

She lifted herself gently into the waiting expectancy of his virile body. Her soul opened for him and his trembling senses told him he had won.

'Oh, Adam. . . .' The soft whispering cry was a plea for love and understanding, but instead of responding, Adam suddenly went rigid. For the very first time he opened his eyes—and then he began staring at her with growing, incredulous horror.

'What in God's name are you doing here?' His face was confused, twisted, then tortured as he pushed her from him and fought his way out of bed.

Lucy wanted to die with shame. She groped for a blanket to cover herself. But it was too late—he was turning back.

'Have you any idea what you were doing?' He gave vent to his rage on the mosquito net; it ripped from its hook and he tossed it aside. 'Do you know what might have happened?' She managed to look scornful—but *he* took the prize. 'I mean really happened, Lucy.' He bent over the tumbled bed and shook her, his fingers biting into her bare flesh. 'Lucy, I'm not one of your young lads. I'm used to experienced women. I thought you were someone else! Someone who *knows* me,' he stressed with powerful significance, 'someone I wouldn't have needed to be careful with!' He intended to frighten her—and, boy, it sure worked! 'And the women in my life don't just take malaria pills.' He shuddered, and passed an unsteady hand over his face. 'It would have been a disaster, Lucy. Do you hear me?' Then his eyes ravaged her and passion burned at his naked soul. For less than a second, an almost tangible cord fused their minds together. For less than a second, they were almost one. Then Adam drew a long, steadying sigh, and muttered fiercely, 'Why you, Lucy? Why you?'

The words were as cruel as a slap across the face. Who *had* he been expecting to find in his bed? His girl-friend—or his *wife*? The thought struck Lucy like a blow between the eyes. Oh no—not that! Why had it never occurred to her before?

'I'm sure it must have been a dreadful shock,' she drawled, mustering all her courage in the name of pride. 'Just fancy—finding me in your bed instead of your wife. Took you long enough to notice the difference, didn't it?'

'My wife?' He snarled out the words, as if he hated the sound coming from Lucy's lips. 'If I had a wife she would be here—with me. I would demand a total commitment in return for my love.' He watched her with a strange expression flickering behind his dark eyes. 'If you think any different, Lucy, it just goes to prove how very little you know about me.'

'Great! Let's keep it like that.' Her heart was leaping all over the place, but she refused to ask herself why. 'Let's agree I don't know you—and you've made it perfectly obvious that you don't wish to know me.' Blonde, bed-tousled curls bounced around her shoulders. Eyes as blue as cornflowers gleamed in the early morning light, and golden tanned limbs folded around herself protectively. The masculine, khaki shirt with all its buttons and tabs only added to her femininity. Why was he staring at her in such a strange fashion? What was he thinking? Was he comparing her with somebody else?

'I'm going for a swim, then we can have breakfast under way.' He had stripped his face of all emotion as he went into the loo to collect his towel. 'Half an hour—okay?'

'But what about me . . . ?' Lucy began.

He raised an eyebrow. 'I thought we just agreed not to get to know each other.'

'I didn't mean . . .' She stumbled off the bed,

keeping the shirt tightly around her. 'You're taking
the towel—and I need a shower, or something—
too.'

He flung it at her. 'Take it. I'll hang the ladder
over the side—give me five minutes to get clear.'

She nodded. 'Where—where shall I go?'

'Suit yourself. But don't come back on board
without shouting out first. I'll be drying off in the
sun. Understand?' he added fiercely.

Lucy gulped. 'Perfectly.'

He went, and she heard him organising the
ladder and preparing for his swim. She stayed well
out of the way, keeping her eyes averted from the
window in the cabin door. It took her five minutes
to reassemble the table and settee, then she collected
her underwear from the pipe in the loo. Thank
heaven at least *they* were dry. Her jeans and shirt
were still a damp heap on the floor.

There was no sign of Adam when she ventured
out on deck, except for his discarded shorts left on
the bench. Lucy closed her mind to the obvious
conclusion and gazed, instead, into the sky. It was
only just seven, but the sun was already warm and
bright, with no sign of yesterday's stormy clouds.
The boat was nestling behind a sharp promontory in
a natural little bay. If she waded ashore and crossed
the jutting out tangle of trees, she would be able to
bathe out of sight of the boat. . . .

Problem was—Adam was already there.

Lucy stood in the protection of the tall, dark trees
and watched his powerful arms breaking the surface
in a magnificent crawl. Then he dived and his legs
and feet shot into the air. Where had he gone? Was

he all right? She gasped as he suddenly appeared very close to the bank.

He rose out of the water and sunlight caught the shimmering droplets as they drained off his shoulders and chest. He stretched and fingered his thick dark hair back into place. A parrot screeched from a tree and as it nosedived the fast-flowing water, he turned his head quickly, as attracted by the flash of bright colours as Lucy had been. He was close enough for her to see his expression, and when he turned back towards her a ghost of a smile still hovered over his lips.

Lucy was enthralled by the magnificent splendour of the man. The broad span of his chest was accentuated by a line of dark hair which plunged all the way down to his waist, and as he began striding towards the bank, the water receded and the dangerous line crept insidiously lower. A flat, iron-hard stomach and firm, tapering hips. . . . Too late, Lucy suddenly realised that he was naked!

She turned around and fled. It hadn't occurred to her! Vines and creepers clung to her arms and face, and she tore them away, wishing she had a machete. She had to get away—if Adam should find her here—watching him. . . . She wasn't prepared to think of the consequences. The jungle all around her was full of laughs and screams and chattering jeers. But she couldn't *see* any of the animals or birds, they were all hidden away, up there in the dense canopy. Her eyes darted everywhere, looking for a means of escape. What had happened to the brief glimpse of an idyllic morn?

She waited ten minutes, then slowly picked her

way back. He was gone—only a few footprints in
the mud showed where he had been. Lucy hung her
underwear on a low branch and quickly slipped out
of Adam's shirt. She was in the water in less than
ten seconds. It was cool and icy and bubblingly
fresh.

Lucy dived and tumbled and revelled in the
wanton freedom. Then she surfaced and floated
along on her back, a smile slowly spreading itself
across her lips. She ran her fingers lightly over the
smooth, cool curves of her body. Adam had called
her beautiful, even if he had been half asleep and it
had all ended disastrously. She should have been
cross, but somehow you couldn't be cross on a lovely
day like today. Nothing mattered, even Adam Maclean didn't matter when it was so deliciously warm
and the water was lovely—and she could laze and
drift and float. . . . He wasn't married. Her mind
drifted pleasantly, and it was all mixed up with the
day, and the warmth, and a special sort of feeling—
rather like being in love. It didn't even seem to
matter that he had seen her naked after the ant episode—because now she had seen him. That made
them quits—didn't it . . . ?

She remembered to shout before climbing back
on board, and when the 'all clear' came, she hauled
herself up the ladder. She cast a covert look through
the cabin door, but he was respectable now, back in
his old tattered shorts. He had hung her jeans and
shirt, and the blanket, on an improvised line to dry.
They were already beginning to steam as the early
morning sun rose higher.

He came out on deck carrying a mug and shaving

equipment. 'I've put another shirt out for you,' he said flatly. 'This lot will take a little while to dry.'

Lucy felt surprised and strangely pleased, yet unsure if she should show it. It was a check job this time, mossy green and fawn. The sleeves were short, at least, they only came down to her elbows, and the slits up the side didn't matter quite so much now that she was back in her broderie anglaise pants and bra again.

He even lent her his comb, and she sat on the back deck painfully untangling her hair. Through a curtain of curls she watched as he lathered his face and unfolded a lethal-looking razor. Her eyes widened as he wielded the dangerous instrument with short, sharp strokes against his cheek and throat. How matter-of-fact he was about it all, yet for her it was a whole new experience. Apart from her father, years ago, Lucy had never seen a man shave. There was something intensely intimate in sharing the little ritual; rather like breakfasting together. Such early morning activities hinted at a night spent together.

Adam wiped his face and caught her staring at him.

'Stare away—don't mind me,' he said, smiling cynically. 'You're having quite a field day, aren't you? Down at the river—and now here.'

The heat rushed to Lucy's face. 'I don't know what you mean,' she stammered, retreating into the cabin before he could say anything else. But he didn't attempt it, and she heard him laughing as he began to fiddle about with the engine. The wretched man! How did he know she had been watching him from the bank? But she would never admit it. Never!

Mechanically she set about finding something for breakfast. Adam had cast off and they were already under way long before the kettle boiled.

Only one more day cooped up on this boat. Soon they would be back in civilisation and everything would be all right.

Lucy stuck to her cheery thoughts all through the heat of another blistering day. This time they didn't stop for lunch, Adam stayed at the wheel, pressing the boat faster and faster against the bubbling current. By evening they had arrived; not that it looked anything special. It was just another bend in the river; trees still grew thickly on both sides. But a jetty had been built and there looked to be some sort of a track. A glorious sunset flamed the sky from pale orange to deepest red. Lucy stood on the cabin roof ready to spring ashore with the line, but as Adam edged the boat nearer, her mind wandered dreamily over the breathtaking scene.

'Jump!'

Lucy was startled out of her reverie and nearly fell. But she managed to scramble ashore and make fast. Then Adam passed her the stern line and she wound a tangle of rope around a bollard.

He cut the engine and wearily joined her. '*I'll* do that—you go below and get some supper.'

Yes, sir—no, sir—three bags full, sir! Lucy ground her teeth, but did as she was told. But it was the last supper she would cook for Mr High-and-Mighty Adam Maclean. From tomorrow he would have to watch his tone. When Felipe found out what Adam was up to, there was going to be a whole lot of trouble. She started shaking some dehydrated stew into a saucepan. Problem was, how was she actually going to *find* Felipe?

For the first time Lucy began to realise her predicament. Clothes and money were irrelevant in the jungle. But how would she cope without either when back in town? She would be totally reliant on Adam, which would mean going where he said, and doing what he wanted her to do.

She poured in some water and stirred the evil-looking brew. He wouldn't—surely he wouldn't keep her a prisoner. Even if he hated her, surely he wouldn't play such a rotten trick.

But a voice inside told her that he was very good at playing rotten tricks. He wouldn't want her making trouble for him. If she wasn't careful, São Marcos might prove to be just as much of a trap as this boat. How on earth was she to make her escape?

CHAPTER SIX

ADAM took one of the mattresses off the bunk and slept out in the cockpit that night.

'Why couldn't you have done that yesterday?' Lucy snapped.

'It was raining—remember?' was all he said, then he was gone, leaving her the mosquito net, and she lay awake staring up into the white filmy folds for hours.

In theory she was supposed to be working out all her problems. How could she get some money—somewhere to stay? Would she be able to contact Felipe? São Marcos was a big place. Would he be staying at the convention hotel? Maybe he had moved on. It was a pity he had been away from Kantara Park when the message about the road had come through. He was the most influential man in the country when it came to the well-being of the South American Indians. Without his help what could Lucy do? Perhaps she could contact the press. *'European girl's bid to save Tukama Indians. . . .'* she could picture the headline spread. And she would have to do a bit of ferreting out herself, find out why the expedition had been brought forward a year. Why had Adam Maclean been chosen? And why did she still feel she had seen him somewhere before?

But the sorting out process didn't go much further

than there, and Lucy tossed around and thumped the pillow. *He* had probably been asleep for hours; but peace refused to come to her that night. Every time she tried to close her eyes, she imagined he was lying next to her again, and her body warmed at the sweet memory of his intimate, searching caress. But how could she have let it happen? It had been wrong, very, very wrong—so why had it felt so incredibly beautiful and right? He didn't love her—he didn't even want her. Yet could it be possible that she loved him?

Of course not. Silly idea. She rolled around some more, pushing the blanket away. What was the point of being in love with someone who didn't want you at all? The shame of it. . . . Gosh, wasn't it hot? Jungle nights were usually damp and chilly. If only she could go out on deck and get some air. But Adam was there—lying beneath a thin blanket.

Lucy closed her eyes and let her mind drift away. As in a dream she saw him holding back the blanket, moving over to make room for her on the narrow mattress. She could actually feel the magnificent body in its complete and total splendour . . . and he was kissing her, deeply, passionately. . . . Lucy wriggled sensuously in her lonely bed. If it was like this in her imagination, what would it be like for real?

Somehow through it all she slept, until a firm hand was shaking her shoulder. It was early— hardly light.

'It's time to get up,' said Adam harshly, and even through her early morning fog she could tell he looked pretty rough. Dark hollows smudged around his eyes. He needed a shave; he seemed to be still warm from bed, and Ludy had the crazy notion of not wanting anyone but herself to see him like that ever again.

'How long have I got?' she asked, averting her eyes from the long, lean length of him.

'Half an hour.' He glanced at her obliquely. 'I'll let you clear up in here while I organise things outside.'

'I'll—I'll make some coffee.' The words halted him by the door. 'I'll bring it out to you, then I'll get dressed.'

He nodded. 'When the kettle boils save me a mug. . . .' The rest of the packing up process was as dull and dismal as that.

They walked for hours, at least it seemed like hours to Lucy. Perspiration trickled down her back and legs. Adam's briefcase weighed a ton. What did he have in it—bricks?

He stopped again while she caught him up. 'Not long now—twenty minutes or so. . . .'

Twenty minutes! She nearly fell down. 'Do you think we could slow down a bit?' He tried, but it wasn't easy for him. He had a natural, long-legged stride and his own pace. And there was no hacking down of branches which might have slowed him up; the track had been well defined—this was obviously the expedition's official route.

They made it to the airstrip ten minutes before the plane arrived. Lucy had collapsed on the ground and Adam had passed her a can of drink. It was warm, but it didn't matter. And they sat in silence, hers was an exhausted silence, until the sound of an engine could be heard above the trees.

The little four-seater plane landed with the minimum of fuss. It always amazed Lucy how the Brazilian pilots negotiated these minuscule strips. There was no room for a slow descent, one minute they were hundreds of feet up, and the next minute practically falling out of the sky. But taking off was even worse. Lucy had devised a method of survival—she simply closed her eyes and prayed.

As the plane taxied towards them and they began to gather their things together, Adam grabbed her arm, and it was such an unexpected gesture that she gasped.

'I just want to make one thing perfectly clear,' he said, raising his voice over the engine as their hair began to blow in their eyes. 'I've brought you this far, without any quibble, without any fuss. I could have left you at the camp—with my men,' he added significantly. 'But if you want me to take you any further you have to agree. . . .'

'Agree to what?' she shouted, while he stared down at her with hard, unrelenting eyes.

'I don't want any trouble—on the plane or when we reach town. You're coming with me, no rushing off on your own. Understand?'

'When I'm in São Marcos I shall do as I please,' she said grandly; the engine had switched off now, the propellers were slowing down. In a minute the pilot would join them and she wouldn't be alone.

'Unless you agree you stay here—okay?'

'You wouldn't, you couldn't just *abandon* me.' She glanced nervously towards the plane, but

Adam only laughed.

'There's plenty of food on the boat. A week or so cooling your heels would do you no harm at all.' He seemed to warm to his theory. 'After all, why should I put up with you? All you want to do is to cause trouble.'

'Then the sooner I'm out of your way the better. Drop me in São Marcos and you need never see me again.'

'I'm not having you running loose. If you come— you come with me. Stay where *I* say you stay. What chance do you think you'll have without clothes or money?'

'You could always lend me some.' Well, there was no harm in trying.

'I could . . .' he shrugged.

'But you won't,' she answered for him.

'That's right, honey. No way!'

'You're a . . .'

His nostrils flared. 'Don't say it—it doesn't become you.' And then he glared over her head and saw the pilot approaching. 'So what's it to be—the boat or me?'

It didn't take long for Lucy to decide. Anyway, promises needn't be kept when they were made under duress. 'You,' she mumbled, and it seemed enough. Adam released her, and then went with a smiling face and hand outstretched to meet their dashing young pilot.

'We shall be in São Marcos by lunchtime,' they were told, when everything and everybody was finally installed. Adam sat in the co-pilot's seat, which he pushed right back to accommodate his giant's legs. The seat pressed hard against Lucy's knees. It was so hot in the little cabin, and lunchtime seemed hours away. The engine was started and the propellers gathered speed until they were a hazy revolving blur. Then they taxied over the bumpy ground and turned towards the waiting line of dark trees. Then they were off, hurtling nearer and nearer the line of destruction; Lucy closed her eyes and went through the usual procedure. It worked—they were airborne. Not long now and then freedom ... Lucy wasn't quite sure how she would escape, but escape she certainly would. ...

There wasn't much chance of getting away at the airport. Airport! That was a laugh. They landed just after midday. Nearly four hours crammed into a hot, vibrating can. Lucy felt stiff and unsteady as she tottered on to the ground, then there was all the unloading to do again before they could make their way to the ramshackle hut called a waiting room. The hard white runway seemed to dance and shimmer in the paralysing heat. Sweat trickled down Lucy's back and she could feel her shirt clinging between her shoulder blades. Adam strode ahead and she lugged his briefcase in the direction of shade. Maybe there was a canteen, perhaps she could have a drink. But the facilities at São Marcos weren't spartan—they just didn't exist!

She sat at a fly-specked table and wiped her damp forehead with the back of her hand. Everything was dusty and downtrodden. The jungle might be primitive, but it was lush and clean compared with this.

Adam had disappeared into an office; he seemed

to know everyone, she had heard warm salutations
when they had arrived. Suddenly realising she was
alone for the first time, she looked around for a
means of getting away. But how could she get a taxi
when she couldn't pay the fare? Maybe it would be
best to keep up the pretext of complying with his
wishes for a little longer.

It was a good decision, for at that moment he
appeared again, ordering everyone about and not in
the least affected by the heat.

'By the time we get this lot outside the car will be
here,' he said, more or less in her direction. After
being in such close proximity to the great man, it
was a curious feeling to realise she was only a very
tiny part of his life.

The car was large, black, an ancient relic hanging
together with dust and goodwill. Lucy dived inside
and sank into the torn and faded leather seat. Bags
were piled round her, then Adam eased himself into
the front passenger seat. No one said anything; the
driver seemed to know where they were going.

Lucy had given the matter quite a lot of thought.
Where were expeditions usually organised from? A
hotel? It seemed unlikely. An apartment perhaps—
or had someone lent them a house in the shabbier
part of town?

São Marcos was just as she had expected it to
be—hot, noisy, cars and dust flying in all directions.
She remembered having read that it had grown up
during the rubber boom, years ago. But now the
colonial type buildings, once resplendent in pinks
and greens, were faded, cracked, worn out and un-
lovely; like an old, ugly woman who had once been

a music-hall star. A lot of the old buildings had been pulled down, and harsh skyscrapers looked like sightless giants as their windows were shaded with inside blinds. The car careered round corners, hot tyres on hot tarmac screeching spectacularly. It seemed that every driver in São Marcos was bent on self-destruction.

Adam didn't turn a hair. He wedged his feet under the dashboard, and hung on to the back of his seat. He was big enough to brace himself all round, but Lucy's feet hardly touched the floor, and she was bounced all over the place. It would serve them both right if she was sick!

They were through the commercial part of the town, Lucy was trying desperately to remember the way, and the houses seemed much better cared for. The roads were narrower, a crazy tangle of high walls and eyeless windows, they drove round a square and passed an ornate church; bells were ringing. Women in black peered into the car as it forced them to take refuge in dark doorways. Then they were nosing their way into a silent, deserted square. Tall trees shaded old, worn flags. The car stopped and Adam eased himself out and opened a massive door in a tall, faceless wall, and the car drove through the arch into a cool, gracious wonderland.

Lucy climbed out of the car and stared around—amazed that such luxury should exist behind a high, imposing façade. The courtyard was a symphony of dark shade and brilliant light; sunshine, white walls and a fountain sliced with blackness by the tall, shuttered house rising on all sides. A balcony around the first floor cast the lower rooms in a cool, mysterious darkness. The eyes couldn't adjust to the contrast. It was a beautiful, yet enigmatic, prison.

Everything had to be unloaded, thank heaven this was the last time, then the old Mercedes reversed under the arch and Adam swung the doors shut on the outside world. Trapped, thought Lucy. But not for long!

'They must be out,' he said, coming towards her again. 'Leave that lot.' He nodded towards the heap at her feet. 'Come with me and I'll show you your room. While you freshen up I'll see about getting us something to eat.'

It had been a very long morning, she couldn't escape without some sort of plan, so she followed him blindly, the house dark and confusing after the brilliant light outside. She had an impression of sumptuous elegance, tiled floors, bright woven rugs, wall hangings, heavy carved furniture, then a steep staircase curving up to the first floor.

Adam knew his way around, he didn't hesitate, and passed several doors before finally opening the third. 'Bathroom's through there,' he indicated briefly with a nod. 'When you're ready come down. Shout if you can't find me—in this sort of house you can easily get lost.'

'It's—it's very nice,' she mumbled, feeling something of the kind ought to be said. Who did it belong to—was it his? But if he sensed the question behind her compliment, he was in no mood to answer it.

He left, and Lucy made a dash for the bathroom. First things first, she could puzzle that one out later.

It was a long time since she had felt so deliciously

clean. The bathroom cupboard had been filled with
jars and bottles, so she had washed her hair under
the shower, then sank into a soothing, sweet-smell-
ing bath. It was only hunger that eventually made
her heave herself out.

The towels were soft and thick and she padded
back to her room, revelling in the unexpected
luxury. But it wasn't so nice putting her old, dusty
clothes back on. Afterwards, Lucy stared at her reflection in the long, ornate mirror. If only she had
some more clothes—or some money. . . . The sound
of voices and people arriving broke her thoughtful
mood. She went over to the shutters and peeped
through. But she couldn't see anyone, the balcony
cut off most of the view, although the door in the
wall had been opened and she could just see the top
of a white car.

Those doors—open! It took several seconds for
this obvious fact to sink in. Then now was the time
to go—they wouldn't expect her down for ages.
Adam would be wrapped up with the new arrivals,
perhaps explaining about Lucy. If she left it any
later he would have passed the word for everyone to
keep an eye on her. It was now or never, and with
her heart beating fast she went across to the door
and nervously tried the handle.

It opened, the corridor was deserted, and on
tiptoe she made her way to the head of the stairs.
Only an ancient grandee, portrayed in heavy oils,
stared down at her from a gilt frame. But he was
beyond giving secrets away, and Lucy heard laughter and the clink of glasses as she slowly descended
the twisting stair.

There wasn't time to wonder if anyone could see her from a window. Lucy kept against the walls, circling the little pond; no one cried out, no shout came. She slipped behind the car, ducking low for a moment, then she made a final dash through the heavy oak doors. It was easy—too easy—the square was deserted and she ran across it and darted down a narrow street. She had done it. Phew! She was free. So why on earth did she feel like sinking on a doorstep and having a good cry?

The road up to the villa had been steep, so now she kept running down, down one dark narrow street after another. Everything became noisier and dustier, soon the hectic town came up to meet her. The backs of warehouses, sleazy-looking shops; Lucy hurried past, eyes downcast, as men leered at her from doorways.

At last she struck a busy main road and instinct turned her footsteps to the right. How quickly elegance turned to shabbiness out here. The house, a cool, tree-lined square were only a few minutes' run from the hot, steamier part of town. But at least Lucy had been dressed for the part; as she plodded nearer the fashionable shopping centre she became more and more conscious of her dishevelled shirt and jeans.

Eventually she found a tourist centre and asked where the Conference on International Aid was being held.

'The Hotel Fortuna.' Lucy sighed; it turned out to be a very complicated set of directions. 'You would like a taxi?' she was asked courteously.

'No—no, I'll walk,' and she smiled, trying to look

Your special introduction to the Mills & Boon Reader Service.
A chance to enjoy 4 spellbinding Romances absolutely FREE.

Four exciting Mills & Boon Romances have been specially selected for you to enjoy FREE and without any obligation. You can meet Caroline, her imminent marriage threatened by a misunderstanding . . . Karen, forced to meet the husband she still loves two years after their divorce . . . Sabrina, tragically blinded and fighting a little too hard to be independent . . . Ravena, about to marry a forbidding stranger to protect her beloved guardian from a terrible secret.

Intriguing relationships . . . memorable characters . . . exciting locations . . . Our readers tell us that the books we select have them 'hooked' from the very first page. And they're a joy to read to the last loving embrace.

The Unwilling Bride
by Violet Winspear
Ravena loved her guardian and desperately wanted to protect him from a terrible secret about his son. But that meant marrying forbidding Mark di Curzio in order to bear him a son.

The Marriage of Caroline Lindsay
by Margaret Rome
Caroline agreed to marry Domenico Vicari to give her sister's abandoned baby a home and security. But Domenico believed the baby to be Caroline's own.

With the help of the Mills & Boon Reader Service you could receive
ery latest Mills & Boon titles hot from the presses each month. And
an enjoy many other exclusive
ntages:

No commitment. You receive books for only as long as you want.

No hidden extra charges. Postage and packing is free.

Friendly, personal attention from Reader Service Editor, Susan
nd. Why not ring her now on 01-689 6846 if you have any queries?

FREE monthly newsletter crammed with knitting patterns, recipes,
etitions, bargain book offers, and exclusive special offers for you,
home and your friends.

OUR FREE BOOKS ARE OUR SPECIAL GIFT TO YOU. THEY ARE
RS TO KEEP WITHOUT ANY OBLIGATION TO BUY FURTHER BOOKS.

ave nothing to lose—and a
e world of romance to gain.
ill in and post the coupon

& Boon Reader Service,
ox 236, Croydon, Surrey CR9 9EL.

ory Cane
t Dailey
a coped bravely with the tragedy of
blinded in an accident. But how could
he cope with a man who offered pity
when she needed his love?

Seen by Candlelight
by Anne Mather
Even two years after their divorce, Karen
still loved her husband Paul. To protect
her sister from the advances of Paul's
married brother Karen must meet him
again—a meeting she
dreaded.

like a 'keep fit' fanatic. But it was three o'clock now—she had been up since five, and it seemed a very long time since that early breakfast of biscuits and the last of the tinned meat.

When she finally found the hotel, she began to be really worried. What if Felipe wasn't there? Supposing he had checked out—or simply gone away for the day? She couldn't imagine the hotel letting her hang around in one of their lounges. They would probably think her scruffiness would give the hotel a bad name.

'I would like to see Senhor Ramirez,' she said with all the confidence she could muster. 'Tell him it's Lucy Blake. It's very important,' she added grandly, and after only a slight hesitation the reception clerk picked up a phone and dialled.

'Room 362,' he said, putting the receiver back and waving a hand towards the lift. 'Senhor Ramirez said you were to go straight up.' It was as easy as that. Lucy couldn't believe it. The lift? Where was it? Ah—over there. . . .

'My dear Lucy!' The tall, elegant Brazilian clasped her shoulders and kissed her on both cheeks. It was just too much, she couldn't take any more, and she sank in a shower of tears against his chest.

Felipe wouldn't hear a word until she was installed in a huge armchair in his cool, air-conditioned room. Her face was grey with tiredness, her hair limp and damp after all her rushing about. He seemed to sense she was starving and he ordered a substantial snack over the phone.

'Now—tell me,' he said, coming to squat beside her chair and taking both her hands in his. 'What has happened?' he asked gently, his eyes kind and dependable. Lucy sniffed and he pulled out a hanky. 'Come, dry your eyes. It can't be as bad as all that. . . .'

'Oh, yes, it can,' she interrupted indignantly. And slowly the whole story came tumbling out. 'It all began with a radio message from your Park. They'd heard that an expedition was coming our way—right through the Tukamas' hunting ground—another great road,' she added bitterly. 'And not next year, but now! And you weren't there,' she gulped, 'and I didn't know what to do. They said you were here—at this conference. So I tried to stop him. Sam took me up river—one of the hunting parties had come across their base. I reasoned with him, Felipe. I *explained*—honestly, I tried everything. But he wouldn't listen—didn't care. So I—so I thought I'd better come and find you.' She tugged at his jacket. 'You'll stop him, won't you? People like him ought to be locked up!' She broke off. He was staring at her in a peculiar way. He was an extremely attractive man for someone of his years. The grey, almost white hair waved back from his face making him appear ageless.

'This is bad—very bad indeed.' He released her hands and got up to answer the door as the floor waiter arrived. 'I have had no notification of this,' he went on, speaking to Lucy over the waiter's head. 'There was some talk of altering the route—but they had not made up their minds. . . .' He was cross—upset. He had spent most of his life trying to bring help to the South American Indians. Now there was this new setback, more land seized from his precious

Park. He moved restlessly over to the bed and picked up the phone. The waiter left and Felipe gestured to Lucy to begin her meal. 'Who—who is leading the expedition?' he asked, beginning to dial.

'Maclean,' Lucy ground out. 'Adam Maclean,' and to her astonishment Felipe put down the phone and stared.

'He is here—in Brazil—now?' His command of the English language was usually better than that.

Lucy nodded. 'Do you know him—have you met him before?' she asked.

Felipe stood up and began patrolling the floor. 'Everyone knows Adam Maclean. Surely you've heard of him? Explorer. Author. Member of your Geographical Society. You must have seen his documentaries on television.' He paused and rubbed his chin. 'He was out here years ago, when the Park first began. But I thought he was in Thailand somewhere trying to find a site for a new dam.'

Now it was Lucy's turn to stare in horror. Of course—that was where she had seen him before. 'Did he make a programme last year about the Nile?' And when Felipe confirmed, still rubbing his chin thoughtfully, she felt cold and afraid inside, gradually realising the strength and importance of the opposition. *Adam Maclean*. Wasn't it just her luck? Everyone had heard about him.

'You had better tell me everything that has happened,' he said, sitting down again and preparing himself to listen.

So she told him everything that had happened since she had met Adam. How she had *persuaded* him to bring her to São Marcos; about the boat trip—

well, some of it! And she gave only a brief account of their arrival in town.

'And he doesn't know you're here—with me?' asked Felipe, sensing there was still more to the tale than her words. Lucy shook her head, picking her way disconsolately through the tempting food. 'How did you get here?' he persisted. 'Where are you staying?' and she sighed and laid down her knife and fork with a clatter.

'It's like this, Felipe,' she began slowly, and she told him about Adam Maclean's threat, and her escape from the villa, and when she had finished a dark, forbidding look had come into his eyes.

He picked up the phone again and asked if they had a single room available. 'It's the Conference,' he said, smiling at her briefly. 'They think they're full, but they'll phone me back.' He pulled out his wallet and laid a pile of notes beside him on the bed. 'When you've rested, go and get yourself whatever you need. And get a pretty dress—have dinner with me tonight.'

'Felipe, you're an angel!' Lucy scurried across to him and planted a kiss on his cheek. 'I'll pay you back, just as soon as I can get hold of my cheque book.'

He gave a very unfatherly sigh and put her from him. 'It is such a pity that you remind me of my daughter,' he said, with twinkling, mischievous eyes.

'You rogue!' she smiled, tapping him lightly on the nose, then the phone rang and he turned to answer it. It was a shame all men weren't as honourable as he.

'We are in luck; they have a very, very small room. . . .'

'It doesn't matter. I'll be safe there.' His eyes narrowed, and she added quickly, 'Bless you!'

She shared her coffee with him. It was hot, strong and tacky sweet; it didn't refresh, but it certainly revived. By the time Felipe had told her all about the Conference, Lucy was feeling strong enough to launch out on a shopping trip. At last she could begin to relax. Everything was out of her hands now. If anyone could get the expedition recalled it was this man.

She stuffed the notes into the pocket of her jeans and securely fastened the zip. 'I'll see you later, then,' she smiled. 'What time's dinner—about nine?'

Felipe nodded and she stopped him getting up to show her out. He had a lot to do in the next few hours, and as she turned to wave goodbye from the door he was already stretching out his hand again for the phone.

It served him right! Adam Maclean was nothing but a no good bully. It was about time he learned that he couldn't have everything his own way. What if he was a big shot? Now that the curtain of memory had been pulled back, she could remember seeing a huge display of his books back in London in a fashionable Piccadilly store. But that didn't give him the right to destroy. The Indians needed protecting; from progress, from civilisation—and from Adam Maclean.

The lift brought her down to the ground floor and the cool reception area was contrasted by the intense heat outside. Cars hooted and screeched and pedestrians began mingling on the busy pavements. She was free—she had a friend and some money. This was the moment to forget about Adam and enjoy her spree.

She found a department store and quickly bought a cotton wrap-around skirt and a couple of tee-shirts, which she changed into in the ladies' loo. Her dusty jeans and shirt were consigned to the carrier bag. Now she looked more respectable—but she also knew it could act as a disguise. It was hardly likely that Adam would be searching for her here. But you never knew with Adam—you could never tell. . . .

Then Lucy bought all the mundane things like a brush and comb and toiletries in general. Some more underwear next, and a pair of respectable, high-heeled sandals. Then it was time to indulge herself with a delicious froth of a dress.

Brazilian women were notoriously beautiful—tall, statuesque creatures, with magnificent figures who always made Lucy feel small, pale and inconsequential. But she was petite and feminine and *they* wouldn't be able to slip into a size ten. Finally she found the ideal thing, thin shoulder straps and low, plunging neckline. It was loose and swirly in a crimped sort of chiffon. It was the palest of pale aquamarine.

Lucy felt thoroughly pleased with herself as she took the escalator downwards. But what about a bag?—and so it went on; she bought a lipstick, some nail varnish and the tiniest phial of her favourite perfume.

Bags and packages hung all round her, and it was several minutes of jostling other shoppers before she suddenly remembered that she could now call a taxi. It whisked her back to the hotel with São

Marcos drivers' usual exuberance, but this time she didn't mind. Lucy was looking forward to having a long, cool bath and leisurely preparing for dinner.

She collected her key from the desk and was told that Senhor Ramirez would like her to join him in the lounge. The clerk pointed her in the right direction and someone held the glass door open as she glided through into the hushed, soothing atmosphere of deep, white settees, cool tiled floor and the shady foliage from lush green potted plants.

She saw Felipe in a quiet corner and he rose as she approached. But when she got nearer Lucy saw that someone else was sitting with him; someone who had been hidden from the doorway by a giant, overhanging palm. She stopped in her tracks and her heart stood still. It was Adam. Adam Maclean. Felipe had betrayed her.

CHAPTER SEVEN

'It's all right, my dear, there's no need to be afraid.'
Felipe took her arm and led her resolutely to a
chair. He pressed her down and she perched on the
edge. Afraid? What did he know? What story had
Adam been spinning now?

She glared across the smoked glass table, hate and
a certain triumph shining from her eyes. She had
escaped; he didn't like that. And he might have
been able to fool Felipe, but he certainly wasn't
going to fool her.

Hostility leapt between them. Adam's eyes flicked
over her new appearance; the swirling skirt display-
ing legs and neat ankles, the scant, curvaceous tee-
shirt, and the elegant labels on the box containing
her dress. He glanced at Felipe and then back to
Lucy's face. His mouth thinned distastefully and she
could easily read his mind. Did he think Felipe had
bought her *presents*? That she was his—his—*mistress*?
Things were getting better by the minute. Let him
think what he liked! She moved sensuously back into
the deep leather upholstery, crossing her legs and
swinging her foot tantalisingly.

'You couldn't have known,' Felipe began, ordering her a Campari without having to ask her choice.
'Adam and I have had a long talk. He volunteered
to lead this expedition, to try and cut through the
northern route. The authorities wanted to come the

other way—straight through the Park, cutting it in half. . . .'

Her drink arrived and she touched his arm in thanks. 'I'm sure you're right, darling,' she drawled, staring adoringly into the older man's face. 'You can tell me all about it over dinner.' A disarming smile enlivened her face. If Felipe was paralysed by her intimate behaviour he was too much of a gentleman to show it.

'Did you have a good shopping trip?' he said instead, admiration beginning to shine out of his eyes.

'I've found the most perfect dress—you'll love it. . . .' and out of the corner of her eye she could see Adam smouldering away in his chair.

She sipped her drink, knowing she was taking a dangerous path, but there was excitement and danger in the air and she revelled in being the leader for a change, instead of being led.

The two men began talking about details, some function or other being given tomorrow evening. Oh, how easily he had won Felipe over! She watched Adam's expertise through her lashes. How different he looked; cool and smooth in a lightweight beige suit, silk shirt and brown tie. Well cut clothes accentuated every line of his masculine shape. Powerfully moulded thighs and a hard, flat stomach did wonders for his tailor's craft. He looked long, smooth and lethal, sitting beneath the moth-eaten leaves of a giant palm. There was something very attractive about the outward elegance when you knew the passion and strength that lurked beneath. If Felipe was overwhelmed by affluence, position and the hallowed approval of the Geographical

Society, well, that was up to him. But for her, Adam Maclean would exist as a ruthless, determined adventurer. And that was all there was to it.

She finished her drink. Felipe smiled at her. 'Would you like another?'

'No, thank you, darling,' she tried again, and this time it worked; this time Adam got really mad.

'I'll be off,' he said, with his mouth rigid and a steely glint in his eyes. 'I'll see you tomorrow,' he said to Felipe in particular—and Lucy in general; and she thought, not likely, mate—not if I see you first.

She watched with a strange, tight sensation as he weaved his way briskly between the chairs. Women watched him, he cast all other men into the shade. Then he was gone and the room felt suddenly empty.

'And what was all that about?' Felipe asked, sitting back like a practised father and crossing his legs.

She tried to smile. 'Thanks for not giving me away.' He was waiting, so she went on awkwardly, 'It's a long story, but it's over now. Come on,' she sighed, 'let's get this gear upstairs, I was hoping to have a bit of a rest before dinner.'

'You would like to cancel our engagement,' he said quickly, 'if you are tired. . . .'

'Not at all.' That was the last thing she wanted. She still had to discover what Adam was up to, and Felipe was the best way of finding out.

'I had to phone him, Lucy, to find out what it was all about.' He helped her gather her parcels and pulled back a chair for her to slide out.

'I didn't realise you would know where to find him,' she said, and now it was her turn to catch appreciative glances as they walked out. After three months in the jungle Lucy had forgotten what it was like!

'I have known Adam for a good many years,' Felipe explained, carrying some of her things towards the lift. 'I will tell you all about it over dinner.' Lucy nodded as the lift arrived and as they travelled upwards he gazed down at her and sighed. 'It is such a pity,' he murmured, 'that you remind me of my daughter.'

Lucy was still laughing when she eventually found her room. Maybe, just for tonight, she would help the attractive middle-aged Brazilian forget!

The evening started off an uproarious success. The dress looked even better than it had in the store. The delicate chiffon swirled down to her calves, suspended from pert little shoulder straps, its neckline plunging front and back. It showed off her tan superbly, all that naked swimming with the village girls had given her an all-over sumptuous tan. She had washed her hair again and this time as it dried she had kept flicking it back with a brush, and now, combed, it lay smoothly back from her face. A touch of lipstick; all she needed on a healthy, glowing face; her brows were tapered naturally and her fine bone structure had already been highlighted by the sun. Just a dab of perfume in all the warm creases. When she studied the final result in the mirror she couldn't help wondering if it wasn't all a bit of a waste.

Yet, when Felipe came to collect her, his Latin

eyes opened wide. 'Now you are not the least like my daughter,' he purred, his rich sexy accent as smooth as silk.

Lucy eyed him up and down; the firm, well kept body and tall, elegant physique. He looked devastating in white dinner jacket contrasting with a tropical suntan. Yes, it had been worthwhile, she decided, closing her door firmly behind her and slipping her arm through his as they negotiated the long corridor.

The restaurant he had chosen stood high on a hill with a superb view of the town. As they walked from the car park, Lucy was fascinated to watch the lights twinkling below.

Felipe was a charming companion; it was difficult to recognise him as the overworked doctor who ran everything at the Kantara Park. He was totally committed to the Indians, yet no one would have thought so to see him sitting here now. Lucy had stayed at the Park for a week, before moving on to the Tukama tribe. One evening Felipe had explained how his marriage hadn't been able to take the strain of living in the jungle permanently. His wife had returned to Rio and the jet-setting life they had lived before. So now he was resigned to a life of virtual isolation—except when circumstances forced him to return to town—like now. Conferences and conference hotels were filled with attractive, career-minded women. And who could blame them for enjoying themselves for a few days with such an attractive, experienced man? And who could blame Felipe? Lucy didn't. If she had been ten years older, she could have become quite serious about him herself.

They chatted about this and that and nothing, until halfway through the main course. Then Felipe dabbed his lips with a crisp white napkin, took a sip of wine and studied her carefully.

'Perhaps you are now ready to hear about Adam Maclean?'

Lucy tried not to appear too eager. 'Not that it'll do any good,' she warned.

'You know the road was planned for next year,' he began, and she nodded. 'They had intended going north—I persuaded them months ago; although that way the country is most difficult—the expedition would be most costly.' He resumed his meal for a few minutes and Lucy did her best to wait patiently. 'But then they began changing their minds—the authorities in Brasilia,' he explained carefully. 'The costs were soaring and the expedition hadn't even begun. They got—how do you say?—cold feet.' Lucy smiled and he went on. 'So it was proposed to come south—straight through the Park.' He paused significantly.

'So where does Adam Maclean come in?' she asked.

'He said it could be done—coming north of the river—but he was the only man who would take the responsibility for such a task. He has been out here before, as I said. He knows the country almost as well as I.'

'And Brasilia changed its mind just like that?' she said sceptically. 'Why didn't they tell you?'

'They haven't,' said Felipe, confusingly. 'Changed their minds, I mean.' Lucy looked puzzled and he went on carefully. 'They are not financing this venture—only if Maclean is successful will they agree to build the road his way.'

Lucy's eyes widened. 'You don't say!' she merely breathed.

'Exactly!' Felipe could tell she was genuinely impressed. 'That is why it is all a rush; he—Maclean—chose his own hand-picked team. He had to come here now, a year earlier than we expected, because he was committed next year, as I told you.'

'Thailand—the dam,' she remembered. 'Gets around, doesn't he?' She laid her knife and fork together; suddenly she wasn't hungry any more.

'That's why he didn't want you coming back here making—er—trouble,' Felipe said delicately. But it wasn't delicate enough.

'He could have told me!'

'He didn't think you would listen.' There was silence for a few moments as their plates were taken away, and when the menus were brought again Lucy was only able to fancy a little lemon sorbet.

'So what will you do?' asked Felipe, when they were engrossed in their meal again.

'You mean—will I go back to the village, help them move out?' Felipe nodded, and Lucy shrugged. 'I don't know. It's pretty disheartening. Although I don't really see why we have to accept either of their plans. As far as I can make out, you're having to choose the lesser of two evils. But why can't we stop *any* road in the area? Heavens, aren't there enough already? I'm sorry, Felipe,' now *she* paused significantly and took a sip of wine. 'I'm sorry,' she repeated, 'but I just don't see it. There's more behind Adam Maclean's actions than he would care for you or me to see.'

Felipe remained impassive, yet a multitude of thoughts were whizzing behind his eyes. 'But you will wait,' he said eventually. 'You won't make any hasty decisions?' She agreed, and with that he had to be content. 'I'm sure you are doing the right thing,' he murmured, taking her hand and drawing it up to his lips.

'I'll do whatever you say,' she smiled.

'Really!' He kissed her fingers and an eyebrow arched suggestively.

'Naturally,' she flirted, and they both laughed— and that was when Adam walked in.

His eyes fixed on Lucy like a needle drawn to a magnet, the shock hit her like a blow between the ribs. Then he was talking to a waiter, looking behind him, obviously waiting for someone . . . and when she saw who it was her heart contracted.

'Small world,' said Felipe, following her gaze. He squeezed her hand, then released it. 'Now, my dear,' he said gently, 'coffee, perhaps, and a liqueur.'

At least the ordering process saved them having to talk, and when he turned back to her again, Lucy was perfectly composed. 'Carmen Mendoza,' he offered, so that she wouldn't be forced to ask about the devastating creature at Adam Maclean's side. 'Senhora Mendoza—a widow.' Lucy's spirits soared—then died.

'Was that whose villa I was taken to, where Maclean's staying?' It was difficult to keep the hurt out of her eyes.

Felipe nodded. 'She is a very wealthy woman, very astute business-wise. I wouldn't be surprised if

one of her companies were—how shall we say?—
covering some of the expedition's expenses.'

'I thought you said it was a private venture. . . .'

'Oh yes, my dear, very private. . . .' He trailed off
and Lucy glanced away.

'I suppose,' she began slowly, 'if you were a business woman and had shares in the new road, then
when the area was developed you would be in a
very good position to, shall we say,' she mimicked,
'make a—profit.'

Felipe's lips twitched. 'You could be right.'

'You bet I'm right!' If they hadn't been in the
restaurant, she would have banged the table. 'That's
the reason Maclean rushed in and took over. He
doesn't give a damn about the Indians or your Park.
He's after an easy buck. . . .'

'Easy?' he interrupted.

'Well—profitable, anyway. It might be a bit
tough going now, but you mark my words, he'll be
reaping the benefit for years.'

'I do believe you're right,' said her companion,
smiling curiously, with an odd glint in his eyes.
'Now, my dear, are you comfortable here, or would
you like them to serve our coffee outside?'

Lucy had seen more than enough for one day, but
the problem was getting past Adam's table on their
way out.

As they did so, he rose from his chair with barely
concealed aggression, his face firm and grim, the fire
in his eyes adding to the impression. He gave them
the briefest of nods, but the introductions were taken
out of his hands.

'Felipe, darling, I had no idea you were in town!'

Senhora Mendoza stretched a heavily jewelled hand towards him. He took it lightly and kissed the be-ringed fingers.

'Carmen, my love, you look more beautiful than ever.'

Lucy agreed with him. She had the clothes, face and figure that only a fortune could buy. It came from a pampered, indulged existence, and that extra dimension that God seemed to have granted to Brazilian ladies of rank and position. She was thirty or so—with dark arched brows and incredible bone structure. Luxuriant black hair swirled upwards, then tumbled down her back in a cascade of—what were they?—diamonds! Her dress was black—the neckline bordering on the indecent—yet with her sensuality it seemed naturally the only thing she should wear.

'When are you coming to see me?' she continued in her deep Portuguese.

Felipe laughed. 'I thought you were far too busy to bother about me,' he said in English, and she smiled and made a little moue and told him she was never too busy to see him.

Then her dark, almond eyes politely hovered over the fair young woman at his side.

'This is Lucy—Lucy Blake—Carmen Mendoza,' he introduced grandly, 'a very dear friend of mine.' The two women said nothing but merely inclined their heads.

'I hope you are enjoying Brazil,' Senhora Mendoza said eventually.

'Very much,' replied Lucy, feeling Adam's eyes burning into her side. She could almost feel his rage as he crumpled the napkin next to his plate. Did he realise Lucy was beginning to discover the truth about all his plans? Then he needn't think all this glamour and wealth could buy her silence.

'You know about the press reception tomorrow,' Carmen Mendoza continued, turning back to Felipe again. 'Adam explained—yes? You will come? Both of you,' she added automatically. 'Everyone will be there, it will be great fun!'

The press! Lucy's eyes gleamed. That would be her chance to expose Adam Maclean for the ruthless adventurer he really was.

Felipe accepted gladly, the time and place were fixed and then they were moving off, and Adam had only muttered a quiet goodbye. But they had to pause a moment while a waiter came past with a flambé trolley, and they heard Carmen quite clearly a few tables back as she laughed.

'So *that's* your little missionary.'

Missionary? *Missionary!* But before Lucy could do anything, Felipe took her arm and firmly led her away.

'You will rest here and compose yourself,' he said, leading her to a seat on the terrace opposite an attractive ornamental pool.

'Composed? I'm perfectly composed,' she said, her head shaking indignantly. 'But don't you ever— *ever again*—speak to me about Adam Maclean.'

'Of course not, my dear, the idea could not be further from my thoughts.' She could always tell when Felipe was lying, his accent became more pronounced. 'Ah, here comes our coffee.' He patted her hand, quite unabashed. 'Have a brandy as well—it will make you feel much better.'

Men! They were all the same. Even this handsome rogue didn't listen to her.

It was very late when they eventually returned to the hotel. Gone one o'clock, and as Lucy had been up since before five, she was practically asleep on her feet.

Felipe saw her to her room and kissed her gently on the forehead after saying goodnight.

'Sleep late in the morning,' he suggested, patting her curls and looking slightly regretful.

'What time is the press reception?' It had all been a bit much in the restaurant and she couldn't remember exactly what had been said.

'Early evening—about seven. It's the last day of this convention, so I shall be kept busy until then. Have a restful day, Lucy my dear.' He had the gallantry not to say that she looked as if she needed it.

Alone at last, Lucy was able to collapse on to the bed, and she stared up at the ceiling—what a day! What an evening! But at least she was safe and free of Adam Maclean. But what about the luscious Carmen Mendoza? She wasn't free of Adam—and didn't look as if she would want to be.

Lucy flounced off the bed and hung up her dress. They would be returning to the villa together, wouldn't they? And what then? Hah! She might be a virgin, but she wasn't exactly naïve. Was Carmen the woman Adam had expected to wake up with? Of course she was—any fool could see that. And he wouldn't have to be careful with her—oh no. That sort of woman was more than capable of giving as good as it was possible to get.

Suddenly she wasn't tired any more, but burning up inside with rage. She stripped off her underclothes and had a quick, refreshing shower. What was the good of all this delicate femininity now? She couldn't hope to compete with that sort of experience. She couldn't hope to satisfy Adam—until she learned how!

Back to square one. She rubbed herself dry with angry, brisk strokes, which only made her hot again. The air-conditioning didn't seem to be running on full strength, the little room was uncomfortably warm, so Lucy lay naked on the bed without even a covering of sheet.

Why, even now, did she still worry about pleasing Adam Maclean? Why did she have a little ache—right here? Didn't he represent everything she had come out to Brazil to fight? How could she be in love with a man when he came from the enemy camp?

The phone rang and woke her up, proving that somehow she must have slept.

'Yes.'

'Lucy?' It was Adam! She was instantly wide awake.

'What do you want?'

'I want to talk to you.'

'I've got nothing to say to you, *Mr* Maclean!' So why was her stomach churning, and why did she feel breathless?

'You don't have to say anything—just listen.'

'No!' She hung up.

That would teach him. What a time to ring, it wasn't even eight o'clock. Where was Carmen? Wasn't she still keeping him company. . . ?

The phone rang again—twice, three times. The

hotel telephonist might think she had collapsed. To save all the fuss, Lucy answered it.

'Don't hang up on me,' Adam growled, before she had said a word. 'I'll be round to collect you in an hour.'

'Collect? I'm not going anywhere with you,' she said hastily.

'Be ready. If you're not downstairs I shall come and fetch you.' And then he had the cheek to hang up on *her*!

She wouldn't go. He couldn't make her. So Lucy lay there on the bed as the minutes quickly ticked by. But think of the fuss he could make—and he would, too. Reluctantly, she showered and dressed in fresh new undies and it had to be the flowered wrap-around skirt again; but together with its matching top it looked like a dress. Last night's sandals were a bit high for walking the town. Where was Adam taking her? Just to be safe she left a message for Felipe at the desk.

'And if a Mr Maclean asks for me, will you tell him I'm having breakfast.' She passed over her key with a firm, significant face. The receptionist understood.

'We do not divulge room numbers, Miss Blake,' he assured her discreetly. And with that she had to be satisfied.

On the stroke of nine Adam walked into the dining-room, looking cool and maddeningly attractive in beige close-fitting jeans and brown short-sleeved shirt.

Lucy had been deliberately long over her orange juice and coffee. 'Would you like me to ask for an-

other cup?' she offered pleasantly, but that was only
for appearances' sake, and he knew it.

He sat down opposite her, the dark eyes momentarily glinting with awareness as he registered
her new early morning freshness. His gaze lingered
on her swept-back golden curls, the curve of her
chin and the neckline of her shirt with a few buttons
provocatively undone. He liked what he saw in spite
of himself. Then his lips thinned and his expression
changed to displeasure.

'I've got two hours. I have to show you something. So perhaps you could leave what's left of that
coffee; it does look stone cold.'

The cup clattered on to the saucer. 'Why should I
take one step outside this hotel with you? How do I
know I can trust you?'

'You don't.' His eyes swallowed her up and the
pulse beating out of him matched the same violent
throbbing in her heart. Why did this man affect her
so much? Why was sitting together at a table such
an ordeal? 'Nevertheless,' he went on, 'you'll come
with me. Because if you don't I shall simply carry
you from here. Kicking and screaming if you like—I
won't give a damn.'

She screwed up her napkin and flung it down. 'If
you want to tell me all about the new road, don't
waste your time. Felipe made it all very clear.'

'I'm sure he did,' was the curt reply.

'And about your other little—affair.' He looked
nonplussed, and she managed to laugh. 'You don't
have to explain to me how these things are
arranged. A little financial aid—a road pushed
through where you want it to be. Development.

Expansion. That's how fortunes are made—I know.'
She took a sip of coffee just to have something to do.
Yuk! He was right, it was freezing.

'We're getting out of here now!' Anger drove him
to his feet.

'Certainly.' Lucy rose to join him with a calmness
she was far from feeling. 'As long as you realise that
my mind is made up. . . .' But he didn't stay to
listen, which was just as well. Lucy's mind wasn't
made up—she didn't have a clue what she was
going to do from here!

He had a car outside; the white Mercedes she had
seen at the villa. He unlocked it for her and she slid
into the front passenger seat, then he marched
round to the driver's side and eased himself down
behind the wheel.

The car left the curb in an aggressive flourish.
Adam moved through the gears like an Italian
racing driver, he was using the white limousine as a
display of his own virility and power. Lucy tried not
to be impressed, but it wasn't easy to keep her eyes
away from his stern, dynamic profile. He drove like a
man possessed, weaving in and out of the traffic. Yet
she was never afraid, only wound up and strangely
excited. They had passed through the fashionable
quarter and the commercial section of town, and
now the buildings were shabbier, washing was hanging from some of the windows. Where was he taking
her? What was about to happen?

He finally screeched into a garage and came to a
jerking halt. They hadn't said a word to each other
since leaving the hotel dining-room. He climbed out
of the car and disappeared into an office. Lucy

peered around; there were some old advertising hoardings on the other side of the road, but the paper was peeling off, dust and old cans moved restlessly along in the gutter. An old clapped-out truck was having a tyre changed, and two mechanics had stopped in their task and were leering at her.

Lucy turned away, wishing she had some sunglasses to hide behind. She felt conspicuous in the luxurious car with her fresh new clothes. She crossed her legs, then uncrossed them. What would she do if one of them came over? Hit the horn! Adam must be somewhere.

She twisted round and saw him standing in a doorway still talking to the person in the darkened room. Her relief was shortlived as he strode back towards her, his steps long and brisk, before bending down and wrenching open her door.

Lucy felt afraid as she stared up into that grim, determined face.

'This is as far as we go,' he grated. 'The car stays here. Get out!'

CHAPTER EIGHT

ADAM hauled Lucy out of the car as she began to protest.

'I'm not going anywhere—where is this place. . . ?'

'Not pleasant, is it?' He locked the car and began striding along the sloping, cracked pavement. Lucy's high heels keeled over more than once, she clutched his arm in spite of herself. She guessed the only thing worse than being here with Adam was being here alone.

'Wait for me, slow down, can't you!' Lucy tottered after him, the path and road turning to merely dust. The track was dry, cracked; the backs of worn out houses glared down at them. Children in torn, ragged clothes, with huge dark eyes, stared at them as they hurried past. The track began to climb and twist its way into the hills. They were right on the edge of town. There were a few ramshackle huts— and then some more; it wasn't until Lucy saw washing hanging out to dry that she realised people were living in them.

'Ever seen a *favela*?' asked Adam, his face more than usually grim. 'I thought not,' he added, when she shook her head. 'A shanty town in any part of the world isn't a pretty sight.'

'And I suppose you've seen them all.' His arrogant manner got right under her skin.

'Enough!' he replied succinctly. And there was no need to say more as they rounded a sharp curve in the path and the whole warren of brightly coloured shacks came into view.

From a distance they might look picturesque— quaint, clinging to the rocky outcrop of hill. But from this close, the desperate poverty could be seen and felt. Lucy's family wasn't wealthy, but there had always been a comfortable house, holidays by the sea, when she had been a child. Food was something that just appeared at set times, clothes had been bought, a degree of sophisticated elegance had been attained. All these images flashed through her minds, as now, for the first time, she felt almost ashamed of her glowing healthy body, of her casual yet expensive clothes, her styled hair and well-manicured nails.

Children ran up to them in clusters, their thin, grubby arms outstretched. She was sure Adam would throw them some money, but he just gripped her arm and pushed her on. Dark-eyed, sullen women, no older than herself, stared with hostile eyes. An old man sitting in a doorway spat when he saw them coming. Lucy wanted to crawl away and die. It was pitiful, but still he marched her along. They saw a dog coiled up in the shade; it had a huge sore on its back and when Lucy moved towards it, Adam pulled her back.

'Keep away!' he growled, putting himself between her and the wretched animal.

Lucy hid a sob. It was just all too much. Why had he dragged her here? She tugged at his sleeve. 'I've seen enough,' she said tightly. 'Please take me back.' He seemed to consider for several moments before turning back.

It took them ten minutes to reach the car, ten minutes of more despair and poverty than Lucy could ever have imagined. As they neared the garage it made the rough streets and concrete buildings look almost palatial. She thought of the hotel and her air-conditioned room. By the time she sat in the passenger seat again she felt a good deal older.

If she was feeling distraught, emotionally drained, it was perfectly obvious that Adam wasn't. His anger had been boiling away inside him all the time. They screeched out of the garage and headed towards the hills again, only instead of taking the narrow, rough track, they kept to the main road out of town. The dust rose in red clouds behind the car; when the rains came the road would be axle-deep in mud.

As soon as Adam pulled up under some trees, Lucy wrenched open her door and scrambled out. She had seen enough for one day—and she had certainly seen enough of Adam Maclean. Let him roar off without her, she didn't care. She could always hitch a lift back in a passing truck. Or, come to that, she wouldn't mind walking.

'Oh, no, you don't!' He was out of the car and catching her up. The ground fell away into a deep, rocky gully. Scraggy bushes clung to the steep sides, a loose pebble shot from under Lucy's feet and she heard it clatter down and down for ages.

'No one runs out on me *twice*,' he growled, grabbing her arm and jerking her to a halt. 'What the hell do you think you're up to? This isn't the sort of country you can go for a quiet stroll.'

'You leave me alone!' Lucy wrenched herself free and glared up at him. What was the point of running away? It would be much more satisfying to face up to him. 'I suppose you think you're very clever,' she began, tossing the hair out of her eyes. She fell off her heel and propped herself back again. 'But what was the point of it? What am I supposed to do? You can't blame what's happened to them on the Indians. There've always been poor people in these South American states—and I guess there always will.'

'Tough, isn't it? And you think you can disregard millions of people as easily as that. . . ?'

'No one said it was easy,' she interrupted.

'Too right, honey. But while you've been studying away in your cosy little university, there have been people trying to do something about it. Something for everyone—but it's a question of getting the priorities right.'

'And we all know where your priorities lie—never mind the Indians, let's make a fast buck with a bit of expansion. . . .'

'Don't you think those people deserve it?' He was getting really angry now, working himself up into a fine old temper. Lucy had seen him like that once before, on the boat, when he had nearly made love to her. But there was no love in his heart now, only passion and hate burning in his eyes. 'An underdeveloped country needs growth and expansion. God knows it's not easy and there are no fast answers. Mistakes are bound to be made, but that doesn't mean that an attempt at *something* shouldn't be tried. Have you any idea of the natural resources of this country?'

'The way they're going, there won't be any natural resources left. Do you know how many species become extinct every day? Hundreds!' she declared wildly. Well, it was a lot, anyway. 'They're chopping down forests—forests that took thousands of years to grow. It's a drastic change in the world's ecology—a dangerous one.'

'There's no need to tell me something I already know. But it's not enough, Lucy, don't you understand?'

She flounced away from him and scooped up a handful of stones, throwing them one by one over the edge.

'It's not enough because a compromise has to be reached. Men like Felipe look after the minority races—and . . . .'

'Men like *you*,' she said for him.

'Yes, men like me,' he blazed. 'Men like me, Lucy, try and find a solution.' He grabbed her wrist and shot the rest of the stones away. 'Look at me—try and understand what I'm saying. Can't you see that those miserable wretches we've just seen need every bit as much help as your Indians? They need homes, education, hospitals, opportunities, and they're only going to get that if their country can afford it. Your Tukama Indians are in clover compared to that lot down there. Like I said, Lucy, it's a wicked world.' He shook her. 'There has to be give and take—on both sides.'

'And where do you give and take—huh?' She glared up at him, the sky, blue and clear, outlining his dark hair. 'A nice cosy contract and a bit of exploitation. What's it to you if the road goes north of the river? If it went straight through the Kantara Park it would be cheaper; more money would be left available to build all your schools and hospitals. So what's the attraction of financing your own expedition to take the road north? Yes, I know all about it,' she added, seeing his look of surprise. 'But if you were only thinking of the Brazilian poor—you would agree to the road going south, as the authorities had decided on anyway.'

'If that happened, if the Park was split in two, it would be the virtual end of the Indians as we know them—and it would kill Felipe.' Now it was Lucy's turn to look surprised, and Adam quickly pressed home his advantage. 'Ten years ago you were just a silly little schoolgirl without a care in the world or a thought beyond your pampered, safe existence. But ten years ago Felipe finally had official acceptance for Kantara—the land was to be preserved. . . .'

'So what happened?'

'Policies change—priorities change. Inflation. Trying to help these poor devils we've just seen. . . .'

She wrenched her wrist free, feeling sick and unsure of everything. 'Take me back,' she said angrily, because anger hid her feelings. 'Take me back, *please*. I want to talk to Felipe.'

At the mention of the Brazilian's name, Adam's face went livid, and as she marched over and climbed into the back of the car, he pulled open the door again and joined her.

'It's all been a very interesting story,' she began,

frightened by the savage look in his dark eyes, 'although I've no idea why you bothered to tell me. What you do is your affair, Mr Maclean, and what I do is mine. Now,' she added, turning a proud, defiant face towards him, 'now, if you'll be so good as to get into the front seat and drive me back to my hotel. . . .' she trailed off as his face twisted with anger.

'You little . . . Don't tempt me, Lucy, I've just about had enough!'

'Enough! Hah!' But before the sound died on her lips, he hauled her into his arms and began kissing her. His mouth was harsh, brutal, Lucy tasted blood, forcing herself not to cry out with pain. She tried to push him away, but he easily pressed her into the seat. Her wrap-around skirt unwrapped itself in the struggle and Adam became aware of her bare expanse of leg.

'Do you know what you're asking for?' he breathed roughly into her hair. 'There's only one way to deal with a woman like you.' He pulled back from her so that she could see his wild, dynamic face. 'You need taming, my little wildcat. And I've got a very good mind to do it right now!'

'I thought you didn't go in for . . .' she muttered fiercely.

'Virgins?' he said for her. 'Forgive me, Lucy, but any man can make a mistake.' His lips covered hers again, possessively, passionately. What did he mean, mistake? But she couldn't concentrate, it was beginning again, the hot, liquid fire of his arousal.

His hand slid up her thigh and she was pushed down on the long seat. Surely he didn't really mean it. Not here—like this. . . . Why, oh, why had she climbed into the back?

'Adam, no—please. . . .'

'Adam now, is it?' He didn't listen to her plea, his long legs straddled her and catching both her wrists he held them pinned on the seat above her head. Her skirt was ripped away and as she squirmed and wriggled uselessly, he began slowly and tortuously undoing the buttons of her little cotton top. 'I've tried reason,' he ground out, between clenched teeth, 'and now let's see if this will knock a little sense into you.' He looked like a man bent on retribution. There was no gentleness in his savage lovemaking, only a wild excitement that drove her close to panic as he ruthlessly stripped her.

Then his eyes devoured the long, supple length of her, and Lucy arched her back and twisted fearfully, but the movement beneath him acted as a stimulant and he allowed her to feel the intimate response of his own body. She gasped, and cruel fingers tightened around her wrists as he began to caress the smooth curves of delicious nakedness. 'If I'd known you were one of Felipe's girl-friends, I wouldn't have been so—reluctant.' His eyes shone with desire and his face was twisted, almost tortured, with an agony of frustration. 'But you're so young, Lucy, so fresh. Why did you allow it to happen?'

'Maybe I didn't allow it,' she sobbed, as if she had been slapped hard across the face. 'Maybe it was nothing more than a cheap seduction in the back of a car—like this,' she managed to add, with a glare of hate.

His breath expelled and he pushed himself off her in a smouldering, white-hot rage. 'Get dressed!' he roared, but she couldn't do the buttons up and his eyes were riveted to the soft curves of tanned flesh. 'No one accuses me of a cheap seduction.' He grasped her chin and forced her to look up and meet his ruthless eyes. 'But some day I'll make you pay for that unfortunate comment, my dear Lucy. I shan't attempt to make love to you again, I promise—not until you beg me!'

'There isn't the slightest chance of that . . .' But the words were stifled as his mouth covered hers again, and this time, instead of aggression, his lips were gently inviting, deep, warm, sensuously intimate. Then he kissed her closed eyes, her nose, and the pulse beating in the hollow of her throat. This was how it had been in bed together; a warmth, a mingling of souls. She gave a soft little moan deep in her throat and wound her fingers into the soft curls at his nape. His arms gathered round her, and a firm hand slid up her back. She was dissolving, melting into him. . . . And then he pushed her away and her heart stopped when she saw the cruel satisfaction in his eyes.

'I think there's every possibility that you'll be begging me to take you to bed. Maybe not today—maybe not tomorrow.' His lips curled. 'But certainly by the end of the week.'

She snatched up her skirt as he opened the door to climb out. 'I won't be here by the end of the week,' she informed him shakily, wrapping the skirt around herself as he eased into the front of the car. 'Felipe's convention ends today, and he'll be returning to Kantara tomorrow.'

'And you're going with him?' Adam spun round and glared at her over the seat.

'You bet I am!' And he twisted back and started up the engine, his shoulders were stiff and unrelenting. She could see part of his face in the mirror; he was frowning and his eyes were narrow with hate.

The car reversed back on to the road in a wide, sweeping arch. Dust rose in clouds, Adam rammed the gear stick into first, and the Mercedes shot forward, only a quick spin of the wheel saving them from going over the edge.

Lucy was flung from one side to the other. 'Stop!' she shouted, and the car bounced on its springs as he was startled into obeying her. Then she opened the back door, got out, slammed it shut, and climbed into the front passenger seat.

'What was all that for?' He glared down at her. 'Why couldn't you have stayed in the back?'

'I get car-sick,' she said woodenly, keeping her eyes firmly fixed ahead.

They moved forward again, more steadily this time. 'Heaven preserve me from women,' he muttered, running unsteady fingers through his tumbled hair.

And heaven preserve me from Adam Maclean, was Lucy's silent prayer.

They drove back to town in silence, Lucy suddenly aware that the whole episode was nearly over. Tomorrow she would fly back with Felipe—she had made up her mind now. It wouldn't be fair to run out on him now. She would get back to the village, start preparing them for their move. If there *had* to

be a road, then Adam's route was best. But that
didn't mean she had to agree with what he was
doing. After tonight's reception she need never see
him again.

When he finally pulled up outside her hotel, it
was nearly lunch time. Their two hours had somehow stretched to almost four. She jerked at the door
handle, but for a moment it wouldn't open for her.
Adam leaned across and helped, and she shrank
back in her seat, frightened of making contact with
him again; frightened to admit what it could do to
her if he did.

The door swung open and he sat back in his seat.
There was no rage now, just a quiet, unconcealed
contempt.

'I'm sure you'll understand if I don't thank you
for the trip,' she said, one foot already on the pavement, poised to make her escape. 'Very picturesque—and a nice try at seduction. But not quite
my scene. I prefer the more mature—more subtle
approach. . . .'

'Get out of my car!' he roared.

'You mean your mistress's car,' and before he
could retaliate she was out on the pavement, slamming the door shut.

The white Mercedes screeched out into the traffic
amidst a cacophony of horns and quickly applied
brakes. Lucy held her breath, but there was no resounding crash. That man was a menace, he ought
to be kept off the road. . . . Then she ran lightly up
the hotel steps, a triumphant smile curving her lips.
That had been a good line about Felipe—and an
even better one about the Mendoza woman. Hadn't

Adam Maclean been mad?

There was a little boutique in the hotel foyer and Lucy noticed a rather nice bikini on display as she went to collect her key. But she didn't reach the desk, instead she strolled over to the little shop. Why not? Felipe wouldn't mind if she spent a little more of his money. After all, what else could she do for the rest of the afternoon?

So she stretched out under an umbrella beside the hotel pool, and sipped delicious cool drinks, while divers sprayed her legs and stomach with icy droplets of water. The apple-green bikini had come with a matching sun-hat, and it was too bright to sit beside the pool without sunglasses. So, suitably disguised, she lay back on a lounger and tried to have a pleasant few hours.

Only it wasn't pleasant, because she kept thinking about Adam—and what he must think of her. Did he really imagine that she would have an affair with someone of Felipe's age? What was he—fifty? So why hadn't she told Adam the truth?

Pride! He had the incredible Carmen to go home to, didn't he? That meant she had to have something as well. Especially after that humiliating walk through the *favela*. She had never thought about anything except the Indians, never considered the millions already living beneath the poverty line. The plans she had first made with John were getting harder and harder to materialise. John! Strange, but she hadn't thought about him for ages.

She moved restlessly on the padded mattress, wriggling her toes and stretching luxuriously. She seemed a very different person, now, from the level-

headed girl with the clear-cut ideas. Since coming to
Brazil—since meeting Adam Maclean, her whole
concept of right and wrong, what she wanted and
what she couldn't have, seemed to have changed.
She was beginning to see that the South American
Indians represented only part of a very great problem. And if Adam was right, even a little bit, that
only made her want him all the more. If she had
still been in London, she would have screamed, 'But
it isn't right—he doesn't love me. . . .' But the girl
she was now realised there was more to attraction
than a conveniently placed wedding ring.

Yet she couldn't compete with the experienced
Senhora Mendoza, could she?

Lucy took very special care getting ready for the
reception that evening. It was being held at the São
Marcos Hilton, not at Carmen's villa. She had been
pleased when Felipe had told her that. The Brazilian woman had enough of an advantage without
having Adam Maclean on her home ground as well!

It was a pity it had to be the same dress as he had
seen her wearing in the restaurant last night. Lucy
studied her reflection, puzzled to see that the overall
effect seemed subtly different this time. Why? Her
tan was a little deeper following her afternoon ses-
sion at the pool, and her hair flicked back more or
less the same as yesterday . . . and then she noticed
the change in her eyes. A challenging sparkle had
appeared in their blue depths. Adam was about to
regret the day he had suggested she was Felipe's
mistress. Lucy was determined to throw herself into
the part wholeheartedly, and Adam could get as
mad as he liked. A saucy smile curved her lips.

There was something rather satisfying seeing Adam Maclean really mad. Her plan was all set. 'Beg him to make love to her' indeed! Huh! They would soon see about that.

It wasn't until they were on their way to the reception in the taxi that Lucy decided it might be a good idea to make Felipe wise to her plan.

'I—I've decided to come back with you tomorrow, if that's all right,' she began.

He turned towards her in the darkness, his face illuminated spasmodically by passing cars. 'Of course it's all right, my dear. I'm very pleased, but . . .'

'But what?' she prompted breathlessly.

'Nothing.' He found her hand. 'So this is your last night?'

'I don't understand.'

He smiled crookedly and raised her fingers to his lips. 'And tell me, my dear, are you still supposed to be my girl-friend?'

'I was going to mention it—you—you don't mind?' she said quickly.

He seemed to consider for a moment, then a suave smile lightened his aristocratic face. 'This has the makings of a very entertaining evening!'

'But you promise you won't tell,' she repeated anxiously.

He studied her carefully. 'No, my dear, I won't tell him. If that is your final wish.'

Lucy leant back against the seat and closed her eyes with relief, then they were arriving, the car sweeping up the hotel drive. Lights, people, laughter. Felipe took her arm gently and led her towards the lift. The reception was in the private penthouse on the top floor.

'Carmen keeps it for visiting business men,' he explained, and Lucy realised with a twinge that she would be on her home ground after all.

'So why is Adam Maclean staying at the villa?'

'Ah, good question!' The shrewd eyes twinkled knowingly, then the lift doors were opening, straight into the luxurious apartment, and Carmen was gliding towards them, hands outstretched.

'Felipe darling, I'm delighted you could come!' She kissed him with more than appropriate affection on both cheeks. 'And this is Lucy—I'm afraid we hardly met at the restaurant yesterday. I told Adam we should have joined you for coffee on the terrace. I'm simply longing to hear all about your little boat trip.' Her English was good—she sounded fluent, yet there was nothing European in the appearance of the dark-eyed Brazilian beauty. She was wearing a gown in scarlet and richly embossed gold. The stiff material moulded itself to her voluptuous curves, the dress had a low, slashed neckline revealing the depths of a magnificent cleavage. Her dark hair was coiled high and held in place by an ornamental golden band. She cast every other woman in the room into an inconsequential shade.

Lucy could easily imagine Adam's fascination for such a fine specimen of a woman. Experienced. Intelligent. They would make a fine pair.

'There's really nothing to tell,' she said, suddenly rallying before the opposition. 'It was just like any old boat trip—pretty boring really. Nothing in the least interesting happened.'

'Is that so! How unlike Adam.' Then her dark,
magnetic eyes took in the slim outline of the younger
woman. 'Is that why you ran away from my villa?'
she asked, with a disbelieving little smile.

'Not at all,' said Felipe, at his most charming.
'That was because she was anxious to find me. Isn't
that so, my darling?' he added, smiling contentedly
into Lucy's admiring face.

Carmen soon went off in a huff and they grinned
at each other. 'We make quite a good doubles partnership,' Lucy muttered gleefully. 'First set to Ramirez and Blake!'

CHAPTER NINE

Lucy hadn't been quite sure what to expect. A press reception—what for? To explain the route? Interest possible investors? So Carmen didn't intend being Adam's only financial support.

Felipe seemed impressed. 'Carmen has done a good job arranging for so many influential people to come,' he confided, as they took their drinks from a waiter especially hired for the occasion. 'These aren't just reporters; that's the editor of Brasilia's leading daily newspaper. . . .'

'Where?'

'The little man with the balding head, over there,' he nodded, and she followed his eyes.

'All this—this glamour, seems a bit removed from the reality of an expedition.' She sipped her drink. 'Why—why bother?'

'To make an impression. Don't be misled, my dear Lucy.' He took her arm and steered her out of someone's way as the room began to fill with people. 'This is as much a part of an expedition as all the back-breaking work in the jungle.'

She thought of the men in Adam's camp—and those others in the advance party. 'I suppose when you're the boss you can pick the cosiest job,' she said sarcastically. Her eyes were everywhere, watching for him, waiting for him to come into the room. Carmen hovered between this one and that, like an exotic butterfly, undecided on which plant to land.

Everyone seemed to know Felipe and he introduced Lucy to them all, remembering, she noticed,
to keep a proprietorial hand on her arm. She received more than a few salacious grins. Sometimes it
was hard to keep the hot colour of confusion from
her face.

'Who's that?' she whispered, during a quiet
moment, 'that burly fellow with the moustache?'

'That's Maclean's number two, the expedition
doctor and supply officer. It takes organisation to
send people into the jungle—and to keep them
alive. Maclean's expeditions are well known for
being run on military lines. You'll see,' he added, as
Carmen appeared to be preparing to make a speech.

'What do you mean?' Lucy persisted, but he
simply pressed a finger to his lips and she was forced
to conceal her impatience.

'*Senhoras e senhores*,' Carmen began, spreading her
gracious smile in all directions. 'We are very pleased
that so many of you could come. Senhor Maclean
has arrived only yesterday from the interior, especially to be with you today.' There were a few impressed mutterings and then she continued serenely,
'If you will be good enough to come into the room
behind me, we have arranged for you to see a short
film of the progress already made by this expedition.
Then Senhor Maclean will explain the benefits to be
gained and will be pleased to answer any of your
questions.'

Benefits to be gained? Lucy was sure she had
translated correctly. 'Who are the benefits for?' she
muttered to Felipe, as everyone began trooping

towards the door. 'Benefits for the Indians, for those poor devils in the *favela*—or benefits for the people in this room?'

'You have been there, to the slum, you have seen?' he questioned earnestly.

Lucy nodded. 'Adam took me there this morning—he was, as we would say, simply trying to pull the wool over my eyes.'

'This I do not understand,' said her escort, gazing down at her with innocent eyes.

'Never mind, old friend.' She patted his arm. 'Let's get this over, then do you think anyone would notice if we slipped away early?'

'I presume you are *not* making me a very interesting offer,' he said sadly, and she called him a rogue and they hung on each other's arm, laughing.

That was how Adam saw them as he stood in the adjoining room, next to the cine screen. Lucy's heart lurched at the sudden appearance of his stern, aggressive face. Then he turned away and spoke to someone; they found seats at the back of the room, and it wasn't until the lights dimmed that she tried to relax a little.

'As you all know,' Adam began, in a voice that touched Lucy's nervous system, 'a road is planned from São Marcos to the new industrial city of São Paulo. . . .' He went on and on, giving all the usual information, with the aid of coloured slides.

Lucy sat through it all, impatiently drumming her foot. Were they all taken in? Wasn't anyone going to say something? Then the preliminaries were over and he began running the film.

It was strange to see the same faces she had

briefly met at his camp. There was Collison, driving a jeep across a gully with the aid of a couple of ramps. And there was Adam, stripped to the waist, heaving aside a fallen tree trunk. Then there was a close-up of his rough, unshaven face. He was shouting out an order, very impressive—but quite unnecessary. Who had made this film—his agent? Lucy viewed it all with a sceptical, critical eye, but when the lights came back on she could see that everyone else had been well and truly taken in.

'Extraordinary fellow,' someone muttered nearby, with an acute English accent.

'He has a remarkable reputation. . . .'

'Did I read about him somewhere. . . ?'

Fools! They were all blinded by the aura of—of—explorer *extraordinaire*. Couldn't they see it was only a part he played, just a way for him and his girlfriend to make a great deal of money?

'Any questions?' asked Adam, in his usual militaristic fashion.

'How long would it take?' 'Where did he intend exploring after he had left Brazil?' 'Was it true that he was being interviewed for television tomorrow?' On and on, the same inane remarks; the women in the room were almost drooling, and he graciously bestowed upon them one of his disarming smiles.

Anger and resentment were gradually building up inside Lucy. If she didn't do something soon she would explode! Then, she didn't know how it happened, but she was suddenly on her feet.

'Perhaps—perhaps Mr Maclean would like to explain why another road through the jungle is necessary at all!'

There was a deathly silence as the whole room turned to stare at her.

'Who is she?'

'No idea.'

'Ramirez's girl-friend, I hear. . . .'

'*Ah!*'

Little whispers sprang up all round, but Lucy turned a purposefully deaf ear. She was staring defiantly at the man out front. He was furious, she could tell that from here, but he was forced to keep up a calm exterior.

'I'm sure I don't have to explain to the majority of people in this room,' he began, with a tight, brittle smile, 'and it would take much longer than the time I have available to talk about a country's economic growth.'

'Try,' Lucy challenged, and one or two people began to smile.

'I did not come here to present the Government's decisions on their own internal affairs. I came here to talk about the present expedition for a road which will help the economic stability for the people in this area.' There were one or two nods, and Lucy ground her teeth.

'Then perhaps Mr Maclean would like to specify which particular people he had in mind. Bankers? Industrialists? The sort of people who drove the cars I saw parked outside this hotel? Or is Mr Maclean attempting to suggest that the wealth of this area will be more widely spread? No more questions,' she added hurriedly, sitting back down again. That did it! The room was a hub of noise. Now was the time to back off while she was still ahead.

'I'm sure we all understand the young lady's righteous concern.' Adam was addressing them all in his suave expedition leader's voice. 'Unfortunately the ideals of youth do not always materialise.' There was general approval and a healthy applause. Of course there was, they were all as bad as he was, but maybe something would appear in one of the papers. He was speaking again; Lucy began to listen. 'I believe Senhora Mendoza has arranged a buffet supper,' he was continuing, almost pleasantly. 'If you would care to return to the reception, I shall be very pleased to talk to you individually out there.'

The room was slowly beginning to empty and Lucy hung back, until Felipe finally touched her arm. Then she was forced to follow the straggly line towards the door. Why didn't Adam go as well? But he just stood there, nodding and receiving thanks. He was waiting for her—fierce, untamed anger barely concealed in his eyes.

'It was a good talk,' said Felipe, 'very informative; I'm sure they enjoyed it. . . .'

'I'm sure they did,' Adam interrupted. 'Now, if you'll forgive me, Felipe, there are one or two things I would like to discuss with Lucy. Here—in private. I'm sure you'll understand.' He met the Brazilian's gaze without wavering as his fingers coiled painfully around her arm.

'Of course, my dear chap,' Felipe had long ago picked up the English idiom. 'I'll be waiting for you outside, my darling,' he added, remembering his role, and to Lucy's disconcertment, he leant over and kissed her. 'Don't be long,' he whispered affectionately, but it was exactly loud enough for Adam

to hear. Lucy saw the dark flush of passion crease
the angular lines on his face. She began trembling,
but Felipe was merely amused; a playful little smile
hovered over his lips as he quietly left the room.

'I suppose you're feeling very proud of yourself,'
Adam snarled at last.

'Not especially. Someone had to bring the truth
out into the open.'

'*Truth!* What do you know about it?' He picked
up the pointer he had been using for the talk and for
a dreadful moment Lucy thought he was going to
hit her. Then he flung it from him, as if he didn't
trust himself either. 'You're not leaving this room
until I've rammed some common sense into your
head.'

'Don't you try and threaten me,' Lucy warned,
edging her way, nevertheless, behind the first row of
chairs. 'There's nothing you can tell me that I don't
already know. You just want to keep me here because you're frightened of what I might say to those
people out there. Right?' she challenged.

'Right,' he agreed. 'Because the mood you're in
can only cause trouble. You're going to get a few
facts sorted out—for ten minutes you're going to
stay quiet and listen. Okay?'

Lucy pursed her lips and looked as if she was
genuinely considering the proposal, but as soon as
he relaxed she made a dash for the door. He was
there before her, turning the key and slipping it into
his pocket.

'You let me out of here—I'll scream!' She beat
furiously against the solid width of his chest, but she
had found out before that it was a futile thing to do.

He caught her wrists and pinned them to her sides. She wriggled, but it was useless, so she opened her mouth and took an enormous breath. . . .

He kissed her, once, twice, her knees buckled and there was a menacing satisfaction in the steely gleam of his eyes.

'That doesn't prove anything,' she trembled.

'Doesn't it?' His attention was riveted to the rapid rise and fall of her breasts. Soft chiffon draped her curves with sensuous precision. He drew her nearer, revelling in the enforced intimacy of her captive body. 'If that doesn't prove something, I don't know what does,' he said thickly, his unmistakable response to her shatteringly apparent.

Then he seemed as disgusted with himself as he was with her, and his hands slid up her arms until his grip tightened again and he picked her up and practically threw her into a chair.

'Now sit there—don't move, don't say anything— and listen.' He grabbed another chair, straddled it, and leant his arms along the back.

Lucy shrank away from him as he bent closer. Move? She couldn't move. Her legs were useless, simply after one kiss. She couldn't breathe. Was this what fear did?

'Now; have you the slightest idea why I'm in Brazil?' he challenged.

'You told me not to say anything,' Lucy glared, after a meaningful and long silence.

He gave a deep, shuddering sigh and ran unsteady fingers through his thick dark hair. He seemed to be doing that a lot lately!

'Very well, have it your way. Then let me tell you

what I'm *not* here to do. I am *not*, repeat *not*, in Brazil to increase my fortune. Senhora Mendoza has *not* financed my expedition.' Lucy managed to keep the surprise out of her face, but to do so meant staring at him defiantly, as if she didn't believe a word he said. 'No one in their right mind would finance a private venture like mine. Her shareholders wouldn't allow it—she's got more sense than to risk her reputation as a business woman. . . .'

He paused, and she forgot all about his instructions to keep quiet. 'So what's the reception for? What are all those people doing, if it isn't because they're interested in making a great deal of money?'

'Lucy, the expedition is only the beginning, can't you see that? If—no, *when*—this expedition gets through, I still have to convince the Brazilian authorities that it would be a viable proposition to put a road through that northern area. That's why those people are here tonight. Do you think I enjoy this kind of thing; the interviews, all the television fuss? But it's an essential part of the whole crazy business. . . .'

'You must be crazy to do it all,' she interrupted.

'Crazy?' he repeated, staring down at her with narrowed eyes. 'Yes, Lucy, you could be right.'

'So you're financing this whole venture from beginning to end.' He didn't seem to mind her talking now.

'Only on a temporary basis, I hope. If all goes well, and the route is adopted, then the Government will naturally pay all my expenses.'

'Why? I mean, if there's no profit, why do it at all?'

'I told you, this morning. If Felipe's Park is broken up it would kill him. Does that surprise you, my dear Lucy? Does my concern for an old friend appear to be out of character?'

'And what about the Indians? I don't mean just my Tukamas, I mean all the other tribes in the Park—what about them?'

'Undoubtedly, a road through the Park would be the end of them as well.' He seemed almost reluctant to admit it.

'And—and you *care* about that,' she whispered cautiously.

'Of course I care,' he murmured wearily, then a spark of something ignited in the dark tiredness of his eyes. 'But not in your idealised, narrow-minded way,' he went on, shattering the slow emergence of sensitive feelings. Maybe they had only been in her imagination, anyway. Perhaps he was simply exhausted after the recent months out in the wilds.

'So if Senhora Mendoza isn't your business partner, why did she let you run the expedition from her house?'

Adam smiled, and Lucy almost caught her breath. He was so handsome, so exactly like a man ought to be. It didn't really matter what he did to her, as long as he did something. How was she going to cope with the rest of her life after tomorrow?

'I'm sure you're the first person to understand there are many types of partnership between a man and a woman. Carmen offered me her house as a friend—we've known each other for years.'

'As *friends*?' Lucy challenged, then hated herself for appearing concerned.

Adam uncoiled himself from the chair and put it back in line.

'And what's wrong with that? Carmen's a widow—very attractive. We're both over the age of consent. . . .'

'Very experienced, too, I shouldn't wonder,' she said bitterly. 'Was she the woman you thought you'd woken up with on the boat? Someone you knew very well, someone you wouldn't have to be careful with?' She flounced out of the chair, frightened by the sudden anger in his eyes.

'Don't you know that you never reproach a man with what he's said to you in bed? Have you any idea how I felt—the thoughts that were tearing at my mind?'

'You mean it wasn't true, thinking I was someone else? Did you make it up?' An unreasoning hope filled her—only to be cast away as he began to speak.

'Of course it was true—Lord, Lucy, what kind of a man do you take me for? I'm no monk!'

'I'd rather not discuss the sort of man you are,' she managed to say.

'Good. Because you're not in a position to judge, are you?'

She swung back at him. 'Meaning?'

'Meaning that as Felipe's mistress, you're not exactly inexperienced yourself.'

It was a shock—for the second time that day. Felipe. How could she have forgotten all about the charade they were playing? So she couldn't deny it, and held her head high as she marched towards the door.

'Please be good enough to let me out,' she in-
structed haughtily. 'I would like to return to my
friend,' and this time he didn't argue. But as she
glided through the crowd trying to find Felipe, she
could feel Adam's eyes still burning into her back.

What a mess! What a hopeless, sorry mess. She
caught Carmen's eyes through the laughing, smoky
mass, and there was a secret, sensual smile on the
Brazilian woman's face.

It was no good, she had to get out of here. Where
was Felipe? On the roof garden? Lucy hurried outside, trying to look as if she wasn't in a rush. The
humid, tropical night felt like a thick, cloying blanket. Moths danced in the ornamental lights, brilliant
flowers tumbled from urns and were offered to
heaven by marble cherubs. A group of people were
chatting away in Portuguese; they smiled, but
Felipe wasn't among them, and she managed not to
be drawn.

Someone was playing a guitar. The press reception seemed to be turning into a party. If only she
could find Felipe. Would he be cross about leaving
early? Perhaps he could simply call her a taxi . . .
The lights of São Marcos blinked up at her, she
could just distinguish the hills beyond the town, they
were silhouetted a denser black against the dark,
starlit sky.

She passed the room where the film had been
shown; the curtains were still drawn against the
windows. Then there was a bedroom. Lucy didn't
mean to look, but her eyes were automatically
drawn to the soft, intimate light. A man was standing with his back towards the window; he had

shrugged himself out of his jacket and was in the process of tossing it on to the large double bed.

Lucy froze in her tracks. It was Adam, who else looked like that? He stretched his arms above his head and she remembered the same tense gesture when he had been at the wheel of the boat. Then a door to an adjoining room opened—was it a bathroom?—and Carmen crossed to Adam's side. She had been carrying a glass, her face indistinguishable through the misty white net curtain. She reached up and touched his cheek, and as he bent towards her, Lucy suddenly found her strength—and fled.

There was no time to find Felipe, she would leave a message for him at the desk downstairs. The lift swished open at her command, and then closed silently, leaving her a last vision of the party before hurtling her smoothly down to the ground floor.

There were no taxis. Saturday was always a busy night. It was Saturday, wasn't it? Funny how you lost touch. . . . She should have asked the porter to phone for a cab, but she couldn't wait in the foyer; supposing someone had seen her leave? Adam might be coming after her right now. No, he wouldn't, he was busy, she reminded herself fiercely. But her unconscious footsteps broke into a trot, nevertheless.

It wasn't very pleasant being out on her own at night. Her heels tip-tapping seemed to accentuate her vulnerability, yet she marched on, trying to look purposeful. It was several moments before she realised a car was slowly keeping pace with her next to the kerb.

She mustn't panic. She could see him out of the corner of her eye, window wound down, elbow resting on the edge. 'Come for a ride, *senhorita*?' It was a thick, slurred Portuguese.

Lucy looked round for help, but no one seemed interested. In fact, there suddenly weren't very many people about. The bright shops had ended, gracious old apartments rose on both sides. Maybe if she ran up to one and banged on a door. But those front doors didn't open, did they? You had to ring a bell, and you were only admitted by remote control.

The block ended, and there was a narrow side road that she had to cross. As she reached it, the car swerved round the corner. It stopped directly in front of her, on the wrong side of the road, the driver leered up at her. 'Come for a ride?' he said again, and that was when Lucy's fear turned to blinding rage.

She hit him, a solid resounding thwack with all her might. For a second shock registered on his thunderstruck face, and then he was wrenching open his door, grabbing at her arm, and she kicked and fought desperately, but it was useless. He had a hand over her mouth—and over her nose. She heard her dress rip and her head knocked painfully against the car as he tried to drag her inside.

Everything in the world swam crazily. She heard the sound of brakes screeching, footsteps, swearing. There was a sharp, resounding crack and suddenly she was free again, but falling, falling. . . .

'It's all right, my darling, I've got you.'

She began fighting again as a man lifted her into his arms. Then she opened her eyes and her swimming vision finally registered Adam's face.

'You're all right now,' he repeated. 'You're safe.' And then she realised that her assailant was lying on the ground at their feet. For a dreadful moment she thought he was dead. 'He hasn't come to much harm.' He sensed her fear and attempted to soothe, 'Just a rather well-placed left hook,' and as he finished speaking they heard the belated siren of a police car.

'I'll deal with everything here,' said another voice, and through the haze Lucy realised that Felipe was there as well. 'You take her home, I am very good at dealing with the authorities.' Now that the danger was over, a little crowd was beginning to gather and Adam barked at them and they shuffled out of his way. He laid her gently next to the driver's seat, but she didn't want to let him go; the world wouldn't keep still, and she could still feel that man's hands on her body, still smell his spirit-stained breath. . . .

The drive was a confused jumble of cool, air-conditioned car, and the strong, reassuring strength of a protective arm around her.

'He—he just stopped in front of me—there—there was nothing I could do. . . .' and he hushed her sobs with a soothing hand on her hair.

Lucy tried to climb out of the car herself when Adam finally stopped, but her knees buckled; she must be suffering from shock, and then she remembered that bump on her head. She clutched at Adam as he swung her into his arms again. There was the sound of trickling water. She was in the courtyard, not back at the hotel. Adam had driven her to the villa.

'I'm fine now, really,' she said, when he had carried her upstairs and she was in the room he had given her when they had first arrived in São Marcos. 'It's just my head,' and she gingerly touched her scalp, winced for her trouble and swayed dizzily.

'Lie there.' He eased her down on the pillows. 'I'll get some water, bathe your cuts.' Then he gently caressed her bare shoulder with the back of his hand. 'I should have killed him,' he muttered, seeing the angry weals on her shoulder where the dress had been ripped away.

'Don't leave me,' she pleaded. 'I—I keep seeing him. . . .'

'I'm only in the bathroom, in there,' he nodded, indicating the door. 'I have to get some antiseptic, some cotton wool.' With that she had to be content, but she was already twisting about restlessly before he came back.

'Can you sit up, it will be easier?' And as she did so, he slowly began undoing her dress.

Lucy stared up at him, confused, embarrassed. 'What—what are you doing?' she muttered, and he gave a reluctant smile.

'It's torn, Lucy, dirty. You'll feel more comfortable with it off.' And she gazed down at the soiled, ripped chiffon; only it hurt to look down, so she just sat there, mute for once, and let him peel the wretched thing off her. Then he bathed her cuts and bruises with the gentlest of gentle fingers. She had a vivid mark on her shoulder, and a long red line across her left breast. She flinched as the antiseptic stung and stared resolutely at his chin. She couldn't meet his eyes; this was all too much. His mouth stretched taut with barely controlled rage.

'I should have killed him,' he muttered again, and she sobbed and coiled her arms round his neck, and as he folded her to him she began to weep. 'It's all right, my darling, cry it all out,' and he sat there rocking her in his arms for ages.

She nestled against the smooth silk of his shirt, realising that he hadn't been wearing a jacket, not even in the street with Felipe. Where was it? Still on Carmen's bed? And instead of feeling cross, Lucy felt rather comforted. After all, he was here with her now, when she needed him most of all, and the sobbing gradually subsided and she began to realise that perhaps this was all the time she would have with him.

She pressed herself closer, and her fingers found their way to the thick hair at his nape. 'I don't want to be alone,' she whispered, and he stroked her bare arm and kissed the top of her head.

'Let's get you to bed,' he said, with obvious difficulty, and she guessed that even Adam Maclean didn't hold a practically naked girl in his arms every day. He pulled the bedclothes back and she slipped her legs beneath. But she kept her hands locked behind his head, and for him to ease her down on to the pillows meant that he had to come down too.

As he tried to pull away she clung to him. 'Lucy, what are you doing?' he breathed, unable to keep his voice steady.

She began undoing his shirt buttons, her fingers brushing against the dark line of tangled hairs down his chest.

'Stop it!' He caught her hands and pulled them away. 'You don't know what you're doing to me. . . .'

'Yes, I do,' and her eyes were soft and misty and the bedside lamp gently illuminated the delicate curves of her body.

He groaned and couldn't resist lowering his mouth to hers. Lucy's senses spun, as he pulled away. 'Darling, no, you need your rest,' so he kissed her nose and each eyelid, but instead of sitting up, he laid his lips on hers again, a brief, butterfly touch, until he was lost in the sweet, intimate softness of her.

Lucy sighed contentedly; her head was beginning to ache, but not enough to notice; she felt muzzy, unreal, then a sharp pain seared behind her eyes. Adam was instantly aware of her sudden tension.

'You little witch—look what you're doing to me!' His face was tortured with longing. 'What's the matter, darling, a pain?' and she was forced to admit it. 'Lie still, don't move. I'll go and get you something.' But Lucy didn't want him to move. If he went away he might never come back again, and the thought of it was more terrible than the man who had accosted her.

'I'll be fine, it's only a little ache.' She clung to him, trying to pull him back, and such seductive nakedness was almost too much for him.

'I'll go and get you a hot drink—some pills. He unwrapped himself from her long, slim arms, and she could feel his fingers trembling.

He wasn't gone long, then he helped her sit up and supported her back while she drank the hot milk and took the headache tablets.

'It'll go off in a minute,' she tried to smile. Why, now of all times, did she have to feel so wretched? Adam was so maddeningly attractive, so deliciously male, and he was here, with her, not back at the Hilton with Carmen. Wouldn't people notice that he had left the party early? But it didn't matter, nothing mattered. Lucy took a deep breath and made one last enormous effort.

'Where are you going to sleep?' she asked, her tongue moistening her lips with instinctive provocation.

He momentarily closed his eyes. 'In my room—just across the landing,' he told her firmly.

'But I don't want you to leave me.' Her bottom lip trembled.

'I'll keep the door open—I'll be able to hear if you call out. Don't look at me like that,' he whispered fiercely, and then he was kissing her again, bearing her back into the pillows. 'I'm trying to be good—you're not well enough. . . .'

She wriggled sensuously beneath him, inviting heaven knew what. 'I've only got a very little headache,' she lied.

He smiled crookedly. 'And I'd only make it a whole lot worse.' Yet his body responded in spite of himself, and as she arched even nearer, his knee slid possessively between her thighs. 'Lucy—no!' He wrenched himself off her and saw her anguish. 'I want you, too,' he said unsteadily. 'You know how much, don't you?' and she nodded, still able to feel the impression of his hard, virile body. 'You're a very lovely young woman,' he continued, trying to calm himself down; trying to control the natural urgency of his own desire. 'You're very desirable, but you must know that already.' She refused to meet his eyes, as he continued gazing down. 'But you've had a nasty shock—and you're not going to be much use to either of us in a minute,' he added, trying to smile.

Lucy propped herself up on one elbow as he covered her with the sheet. Then, as he began tucking his shirt back in the waistband of his trousers, she said, 'What do you mean—what have you done to me?' Everything started slipping out of focus; those headache pills must be pretty strong.

Adam towered over her, his image swam. 'Close your eyes, don't fight it.'

Lucy could have cried out with frustration as the truth suddenly dawned. He had fooled her, tricked her, right up to the end. Did he want to get back to the party and Carmen? Was that why the wretched man had given her sleeping pills?

CHAPTER TEN

IT took Lucy a long time to wake up the following morning. She had the mother and father of all headaches, and it was difficult to focus. Eventually she ascertained that her tiny wristwatch was showing a quarter past nine. For a moment she thought she must be really ill, then she remembered Adam and the sleeping tablets, and fighting to keep her eyes open she struggled out of bed.

Yuk! Her reflection in the bathroom mirror made her feel worse, if that was possible. Her eyes were puffy, half closed; she looked very pale under her tan, which seemed to give it a yellowy tinge. But worst of all was the numbness of her brain, her dreadful thirst and the hammers pounding away in her head.

She splashed her face with water, but that didn't do much good, so she slipped off her pants and stood under the shower. The icy blast took her breath away, but she clenched her teeth and stuck it out. After ten minutes Lucy stepped out feeling a little more able to cope with the day. At least, now she could begin to think.

Sitting on the bathroom stool, she began patting her hair dry, very, very carefully. Her head still ached and she felt stiff and sore about the shoulders. The scratch across her breast was quite nasty; she wondered if her assailant had been wearing a ring.

It wasn't until she came out from under her

canopy of towelling that she realised there was nothing for her to wear. She padded back into the bedroom to make sure, but the chiffon dress had gone, and there was only one sandal; she must have lost the other one in the struggle. Pity. But now what? She opened the wardrobe door and found two robes hanging inside. How accommodating! Senhora Mendoza thought of everything. Lucy slipped on the feminine version, it was creamy silk, short, wrap-around kimono style, then she tied the sash and fingered her hair into place. The dressing-table mirror showed a slight improvement; she appeared to be fresh and sparkling, on the outside at least.

Now what? She sat back on the top of the bed and propped a pillow behind her. The house was silent, but surely people would be about by now? Felipe must be worried. Had Adam phoned to tell him how she was? And slowly, very slowly, the whole of the previous evening came tumbling back. The reception . . . and hadn't she stood up and made a bit of a fuss? And then Adam in the bedroom with Carmen. . . . She had run away—that dreadful man! Lucy shuddered and hugged herself. And afterwards, Adam. . . . And hadn't he kept calling her darling? Most of the rest of it was still rather a haze. She had been a bit possessive, she remembered. Hadn't she kept clinging to him?

Whatever must he think of her? It was all coming back. Adam putting her to bed, taking off her dress. . . . She didn't want to think beyond that. Strange what you did in a state of shock. Only nothing had happened, had it? And instead of feeling relieved, she felt illogically angry. Hadn't she practically pleaded with him to spend the night with her? And he had dared to refuse, simply so that he could get back to his wretched party and *that* woman. Hadn't he said he would leave the door open so that he would hear her if she called? Well, there it was, closed. She stumbled over to it and peered out. Just as she thought, the door across the landing was closed as well.

Cheek? How dared he reject her! Lucy took a deep breath; she was going to find some clothes and get out of here. Felipe would be leaving at midday and she was going to make sure she was on the plane as well.

Her bare feet made no sound as she tiptoed down to the cool, tiled hall. Rooms led from rooms circling the courtyard; a drawing room, a room with a grand piano, a dining room with unused places still set. At last she came to a kitchen. She could hear someone moving about, probably a maid or the housekeeper, with luck. Only it wasn't; it was a six-foot, dark-eyed explorer, looking as smooth and suave as a politician.

'You're up early.' Adam's voice was non-committal. 'How do you feel?'

Lucy wound a strand of hair behind her ear so that he shouldn't see the unwilling attraction in her eyes. He was wearing biscuit-coloured trousers, superbly cut to accentuate all the right places! His shirt was silk, and he was wearing a tie.

'Where are you going?' she asked, just for something to say.

'The television studios—for the interview.'

'Oh!' she muttered, suddenly remembering. 'Yes!'

He stood with a coffee percolator in one hand and a mug in the other, staring at her strangely, almost as if he expected her to disappear. 'You'd better sit down. There was no need to get up—you could have rung.'

'You mean there's room service in this place as well?'

He smiled briefly as she pulled out a chair. 'Would you like some?' he asked, waving the percolator, and she nodded, then winced. 'Headache?'

'Yes—and a rather large bump.'

He came across and had a look, and it hurt as he parted her hair.

'It's all right, the skin isn't broken. I'll just get you something for your head.'

He disappeared, and the coffee was bubbling away before he came back. He put the pills on the table and fetched a glass of water. Then he noticed her suspicion, and said, 'They're only aspirin—honestly.'

He busied himself with the coffee and Lucy sat there feeling awkward, unsure, yet she couldn't bring herself to go away. He was too wary, too cautious, for her comfort. Almost as if he was up to something. But perhaps he was remembering last night as well.

He began frying himself ham and eggs, and when they were ready he gathered everything up to take into the dining room. There was orange juice already in there, and freshly baked rolls. But Lucy didn't want any, she just sipped away at her coffee while Adam tucked in.

'My dress has gone,' she began quietly, 'and I only seem to have one sandal.'

'Felipe is sending over some of your things from the hotel. Your dress is being mended.'

'What—what happened about . . . ?'

'The man? The police are going to prosecute him for drunken driving. Felipe thought you wouldn't want to press charges.'

'No! The sooner it's all over the better.'

'There's nothing more for you to worry about.' He pushed his plate away and she watched as he spread conserve on the rest of his roll. His movements were sharp, precise. She seemed aware of the merest detail. Everything about him was infinitely precious.

'Where's Carmen?' she said, hiding her feelings.

Adam glanced at his watch. 'Still in bed. The reception ended quite late. I don't expect she'll surface for an hour or so yet.'

For fifteen minutes they continued an awkward, stop-go conversation. Every so often Adam would look at his watch, aware that he had to leave for the studio, yet he poured himself a second mug of coffee and asked her how her head was feeling now.

'So-so! I'd—er—better go back to my room and wait for my things to arrive,' she said, as he came to the end of his drink.

He put the mug down on the little mat and his dark, watchful eyes didn't leave her face.

'Lucy—about last night . . .'

Her heart thumped. 'Yes, I'm sorry—I should have thanked you for rescuing me. How—how did you know?'

'Felipe saw you leave—he asked me to get the car out. But I didn't mean that.' He threw down his napkin and came round to her side of the table. 'I mean afterwards—upstairs. . . .'

'Oh—*that*!' She tried a little laugh, but it didn't sound quite right. 'I—I was practically delirious,' she floundered, 'I don't remember much, actually.'

'Yes, you do.' He bobbed down in front of her and took both her hands in his. 'You remember it all, there's no need to deny it. It isn't wrong, Lucy, we just can't help ourselves. But the question is, what are we going to do about it?'

'I don't know what you mean. I was upset last night—I didn't want to be alone. . . .' But she didn't get any farther, because he was standing up, gathering her into his arms, and very, very gently kissing her. His body felt warm and enfolding, and Lucy melted.

She broke away easily, he wasn't holding her by force. 'I suppose I am attracted to you—but,' she moistened her lips, 'well, I'm not really interested in a wild couple of days. That's not my scene, as they say.'

His stern face showered her with assurances. 'And neither is it mine. Lucy darling, I want you with me today, tomorrow—next week—next year. Come to Thailand with me,' he urged, running impatient hands along her shoulders and down the smooth silken material covering her arms. 'I don't want you out of my sight,' and when he paused and gazed down at her, there was such longing and desire in his eyes that Lucy's heart stood still.

'You can't be serious!' Thailand—being with him next year. It was all a dream, perhaps she was hallucinating after her accident. He couldn't be saying this, looking like that. Not after all the agony of wanting him. . . .

'Never more serious. Darling, are you listening to me?' He tilted her chin up. 'I want you—I want to make love to you,' he breathed huskily. 'I want to wake up every morning and find you next to me. . . .'

'You could have woken up this morning,' she whispered secretly.

'Don't remind me.' An agony of frustration passed over his face. 'Darling, you were the most beautifully provocative little witch—do you know that? You were driving me wild—if you only knew what a sacrifice it was to leave you there!'

'Then why?'

'Because you'd had a nasty shock; you were frightened and upset—and I was angry, very, very angry. When I make love to you, tonight,' he reminded her firmly, 'I want there to be only you on my mind.' A clock somewhere began striking ten. 'Lucy, sweetheart, I have to go, the car will be here for me in a minute. But don't go.' His grasp tightened. 'Wait for me to come back. I want our doctor to take a look at you. You should rest.'

Lucy thought she must surely die with happiness at so much love and concern. 'But what about yesterday—at your talk, I said such dreadful things—in front of all those people.'

'Yes, didn't you?' he interrupted. 'We'll sort out our differences after we've sorted out our other little problem.'

'What's that?' she smiled up at him.

'The problem of keeping my hands off you until tonight.' He kissed her once, twice, frantically, frustratingly, but something wasn't right; through a giddy haze of longing, Lucy sensed there were still many things left unsaid.

'What about Carmen? Surely we just can't . . .'

'You're right.' He pulled himself away and firmly tightened her belt. 'It wouldn't be quite the thing to stay here. I have a friend who has a chalet in the hills. I'll give him a ring when I get back—we 'll go there tonight. Darling,' he kissed her again, 'I really must go.'

'I didn't mean that.' She clung on to him and he didn't seem to mind. 'I mean what about *her*—and you?'

'Oh—*that*!' Now it was his turn to say it. 'Carmen's a very understanding lady. We've been friends, on and off, for years. All things come to an end sooner or later. I've never told her I love her— that's what counts.'

Lucy waited, to give him time to say that he loved her, instead. But he didn't—and something inside her died.

'You're—you're not asking me to marry you, are you?' she said in a tiny voice. And he dropped his hands from her shoulders and took a couple of steps back.

'*Marriage!*' The word was surprise, shock and denial all in one breath. 'Lucy darling—listen to me.' Strong fingers raked through his hair, but she wasn't listening, she didn't want to listen, she didn't want to stay and see him groping for excuses.

'It's all right—you don't have to explain. Pretty old-fashioned idea, isn't it, for a man of the world like you.'

'Lucy!'

But she wasn't there to hear more than that, he

bare feet raced back through the maze of rooms and up, up the curving marble stairs. For a second or two she thought he was running after her, but by the time she reached the landing she realised that no hurrying footsteps were echoing across the hall. But she ran on anyway, desperate to get into her room before the tears came. As she reached it a door opened opposite. Adam's door—only it was Carmen who came out. Carmen in a hastily tied dressing gown and tumbled, dishevelled hair. Coming out of Adam's bedroom! After last night! In spite of what he had just said downstairs!

That did it. Lucy dived into her room, slammed the door and locked it. How dared he make her such a proposition? What kind of a girl did he take her to be? She threw herself on the bed, almost crying out with the resulting stab of pain in her head. She rolled over on to her back and threw an arm over her eyes. Then she realised exactly what sort of girl Adam took her to be. The sort of girl whom Felipe would choose for his mistress.

But even that wasn't really an excuse. If Adam had loved her—*really* loved her—then it wouldn't have mattered what she had done before. It was then that she heard the studio car arrive, and a short, sharp command in Adam's powerful voice. The car started up again and drove slowly out of the courtyard. So that was the end of that, then. The enormity of what she was losing was almost impossible to bear.

Her clothes arrived soon afterwards; a maid brought them up and said that Senhora Mendoza was taking coffee on the terrace and would be pleased if Lucy could join her.

It wasn't an easy interview. Just how much did the elegant Brazilian know? 'Thank you for letting me stay here,' Lucy began wearily, easing herself into another wicker chair.

Carmen shrugged lazily. 'It is nothing—you are feeling better now? That man——' her full lips twisted, 'whipping is too good; you were fortunate.' She put her little cup on the table and leaned back in her chair. Tight white trousers covered shapely legs, a loose, multi-coloured silk shirt was buttoned low, and a matching scarf had been wound round her head, turban style.

'I was wondering if I could make a phone call,' Lucy said, after a few minutes. 'Felipe is flying back to Kantara this afternoon, I think he's leaving at midday. I wouldn't want him to go without me.'

An expressive, thick dark eyebrow arched above her sunglasses. 'So—you are not accepting Adam's offer.'

'I don't know what you mean.' Lucy could feel herself going pink.

'You think he does not tell me his little plan? Always it is the same. For a while he finds someone else, very young, very pretty—they do not usually resist him.'

'I happen to find Adam Maclean extremely easy to resist,' Lucy replied angrily.

'Are the English always so—so cold?' Carmen asked bluntly.

'You know Adam—you tell me!'

Carmen smiled indulgently. 'So you are returning with Felipe.'

'That's right.' Lucy put her cup next to the other one. She couldn't drink any more, she noticed her hands were trembling; sitting here with this woman it was hardly surprising. 'If you don't mind, I think I'd better try and contact him. Thank you for the coffee—and the accommodation.'

'You do not sleep with Felipe, do you.' It wasn't a question, and it pulled Lucy up short.

'I—I thought it was common knowledge,' she edged warily.

'But I am not of the common stock,' Carmen informed her graciously.

'Adam believes it.'

She shrugged. 'In such a case, Adam cannot judge. But I am right, am I not? You are not Felipe's type. A rogue he may be, but in all the years I have known him, he has never been attracted to girls fresh from the cradle.'

'Maybe he thought it was time he had a change.' Lucy was quite determined that the woman shouldn't get the better of her.

'It's quite all right—I shan't tell Adam. Your secret is quite safe with me.'

Insufferable woman! Adam was welcome to her. They made a fine pair. Lucy finally found a phone and managed to get through to the hotel. Felipe sounded surprised to hear from her, but after several moments of pleading he promised to wait for her.

'How long will you be?'

She was getting a bit fidgety in case Adam came back. 'I'm leaving right now.' And for once there was no problem finding a taxi.

'I could drive you,' Carmen protested, but Lucy had seen enough of her to last a lifetime. Then it was the usual fifteen-minute screech through the town, being flung from one side of the cab to the other. By the time she reached the hotel, her head was bursting again.

'You must lie down. Try and eat a light lunch. I shall have something sent to your room.' Felipe had been waiting for her in the foyer, and it was blissful to have him smooth all the problems out of her way.

'But the plane . . .'

'I have delayed it until two o'clock.'

'You mustn't—we have to leave now.'

The lift arrived and they couldn't resume their conversation until they reached her room. The blinds were already drawn, and Felipe led her firmly towards the bed.

'You will rest, it is not yet twelve o'clock. I do not wish to have you ill on the journey.' And that was all he said. No questions, no talk of last night—or Adam. He wrung out a flannel and placed it coolly on her forehead. 'I will get the hotel doctor to prescribe something for you.'

Lucy had a shrewd suspicion that he was deliberately delaying thing, as if he was giving Adam time to return from his interview. But Lucy knew he wouldn't come. What for? There was nothing else to say. Eventually, rested, dosed with more aspirin, and hiding behind dark glasses, Felipe decided it was time to leave.

If he had imagined that Adam would be waiting at the airport, he was disappointed. The supply plane for Kantara was a large, ramshackle affair

looking as if it had been made with dustbin lids
riveted together. It sat on the tarmac, its nose point-
ing towards the sky, and the gangway between the
seats was a steep obstacle course. Felipe had
dropped his role of errant lover, and sat quietly
beside her, adjusting his lap-strap. She was grateful
for the privacy; when your world was falling apart,
you couldn't make polite conversation.

The trip was uneventful, after she became used to
the noise and rattling, and had decided that maybe
the old crate wouldn't fall out of the sky on this trip.
They reached the river and followed it upstream,
its dark, muddy water coiling familiarly, hundreds
of feet below. Three, four days ago, was that all?
and she had been down there somewhere, with
Adam. . . . She searched for a sight of the little boat
beside the jetty. But that was ridiculous, it was a long
river, the spot was probably miles away from here.

They followed the river until a tributary broke
away on the port side and they altered course to
follow the new, thinner waterway. They saw a circle
of native huts in a clearing, Felipe stirred restlessly,
and Lucy realised how much he was longing to get
back.

'Not long now,' she said, attempting to be cheer-
ful, and he took her hand and squeezed it; she had
to turn away quickly so that he shouldn't see the
sudden tear roll from her eye.

It was lovely to be back. They climbed down, stiff
and tired from their journey; the sun was already
beginning to sink and the sky had the makings of a
superb sunset. A group of native children ran up to
greet Felipe, his Dutch nurse, who ran the hospital,

came forward with her plump, stoic smile. Then the radio operator-cum-general factotum, and a young native tribesman, his brown skin streaked with red and yellow. Some of them knew Lucy, and she was touched and smiled at, and she dished out the expected sweets. For a while it was like old times, and she wished she could stay here and be part of it all for ever. But when all the unloading was done, a meal eaten, and Lucy had prepared a spare bed for the pilot in the hospital, she wandered back to Felipe's bungalow and found him swinging in a hammock on the veranda.

'He had the whole place to choose from,' she said lightly, climbing the steps and perching on the handrail. 'Everyone must be very healthy, it's the first hospital I've come across with no patients.'

'They won't stay—especially when I'm not here.' His voice was so quiet that it was difficult to hear above the symphony of night noises. It sounded as if a colony of frogs was out there somewhere practising their scales. 'Have you decided what you're going to do?' he asked, filling a pipe and fishing in his pocket for matches. She had forgotten he smoked when he was at Kantara; perhaps the pipe wouldn't fit in with his bright-lights image. In loose-fitting clothes he looked older, his face more strained. The match flared and the lighting-up process gave her time to think.

'I'll—go back to the village, if that's all right,' she said after a while. 'If you don't mind lending me your boat and someone to bring it back.'

'I would prefer you to stay here for a few days, until your headaches have stopped—until you're feeling much better.'

'Felipe, it won't make any difference.' She picked at the seam running down the leg of her jeans. 'I know what you're thinking—you think that Adam will want to see me.' She paused and smiled at him—this was difficult. 'But he won't. We've already had a talk and there's nothing more to say.'

'He does not care. . . ?'

'Oh, he *cares* all right. Or so he says.' Felipe's eyes widened and she stumbled on, trying to explain. 'He wants me to go away with him—and to go to Thailand next year. But . . .'

'Ah, I see—it is *you* who do not care.'

'I do, I—do,' she said, more quickly than was necessary. 'Very much, Felipe, but I don't know if I can live his kind of life.'

'You mean the expeditions, the travelling? I thought you would have enjoyed all that.' He drew deeply on his pipe while she waved a moth out of the way.

'It isn't that. He—he hasn't said he loves me, or anything.'

'He does not offer marriage, is that it?' he asked bluntly. Lucy nodded and he took the pipe out of his mouth and pursed his lips. 'And it is important to you—the piece of paper. You think it makes a man feel differently?'

'It isn't just the paper. I mean, it isn't as if he hasn't done this kind of thing before. Oh, I don't know. I don't seem to know anything these days.'

'When there is much to gain, there is also much to lose. Living takes courage, my dear? And Lucy lay awake all night hearing the quiet pronouncement.

But there was more to it than Felipe's easily

spoken theory. If living took courage, then loving took courage. And if Adam couldn't commit his love, then neither would she.

CHAPTER ELEVEN

THE Maclean affair was not spoken of again, although the expedition itself was common talk at mealtimes. The pilot flew out after breakfast the following morning and Lucy accepted the offer of remaining at the post for a couple of days. Her headaches soon trailed off, but her appetite was poor and she lost a bit of weight. By Tuesday evening she was feeling restless, uneasy; she wanted to get back to the Indian village, to feel busy again, needed. So she went in search of Felipe to ask if the boat could take her tomorrow.

He was in the office, listening to some crackly chatter on the radio.

'It's the expedition—the base camp having their daily report from the advance party.'

'Are they that close?' Lucy said, in alarm.

'Not really—it depends on the atmospherics. There—look on the wall chart, you can see.' Above the desk there was a map of Kantara, with little flags depicting the tribes already scattered within the Park. There were also several marked that were outside the boundary, her Tukamas were one of them. Their village, north of the river, was marked in red, the proposed route of Adam's expedition had been pencilled in, only fifteen or so miles further away. Lucy knew that a red marker meant that this was the next village in most danger. Now it was up to them all to persuade the Tukamas to move south, right into the Park. The sooner she returned to them, the better.

Lucy wasn't very good at reading maps. 'Where's the base camp?'

Felipe pointed to a spot on the river. 'And there's where their planes land, the jetty would be nearby, somewhere about here.' It didn't look very far, but Lucy remembered the long, hot walk, loaded with gear.

'And the advance party?'

'Hard to tell. At the rate they're going, probably fairly close to the Tukama village by now.'

'I suppose it is more or less certain that his plans will be adopted,' she said, as a last vain hope.

'We had better hope that it is,' Felipe surprised her by saying. 'Shall I show you the alternative?' and he picked up a pencil and drew a line straight across the map from east to west, leaving the post and the southern half of the Park in complete isolation from the rest.

'I'll leave first thing in the morning,' she said.

He nodded. 'I'll have the boat loaded tonight.'

It had taken an hour to fly over the twisting mesh of tributaries, but it took Lucy three days to wind her way back in the boat. She had two companions, a little ageless Brazilian who had been at the Park almost as long as Felipe, and one of the young tribesmen from a nearby village, so there was nothing for Lucy to do all day, except try and keep out of the sun.

They slept in hammocks beside the river each

night, Lucy trying to contribute something to the cooking of the evening meal, but she was usually more hindrance than help, and in the end decided to keep out of the way. On the fourth morning they nosed their way out into the main, fast flowing river. Lucy gazed for a moment upstream. The last time she had travelled that way had been with Sam. She hadn't known then what had been waiting for her; now her life would never again be the same.

But they didn't turn to port, instead they headed downstream, gaining speed in the strong current. By the end of the day she would be home.

The little two-roomed chalet, built on stilts, had been her home for the past three months, and there would be some comfort in returning to its spartan familiarity. She began to wonder what had been happening while she had been away. Had the baby been born? Had the men had good hunting? The last day on the river acted as a gradual transition between one life and the next. Yet the ache never left her. At times she wanted to scream at them, 'Turn the boat back!' She could get the next supply plane back to São Marcos. She even imagined herself running up to Adam, telling him she had changed her mind; she could hear his cry of delight, imagine his embrace, imagine the complete surrender to his invasion. . . .

Yet she never gave the command; the boat sped on, by evening she recognised the familiar bend of the river. Fires were lit, there was the smell of succulent, roasting meat. It was almost as if they were expecting her.

Sam was the first to greet her. He clasped her

arms as she stumbled ashore. After four days in a boat she felt a bit unsteady on firm ground. Then there were hugs all round, kisses for the children, and she dished out fishing hooks and sweets, and was dragged off to see the new baby; it was a boy, everyone was thrilled. Only then did they allow her to go indoors, but not before she had agreed to come to the festivities they were arranging that night.

'I need a bit of a rest,' she told Sam, in her best Portuguese. 'Come and see me when you're ready to start.'

He smiled, his teeth gleaming, and the dark, swinging fringe making him look more wicked than ever.

What was he up to? It was time he got married. And, with a smile still hovering on her lips, she strolled wearily over to the bungalow and climbed the steps. The boxes of supplies they had brought with them had been piled up and she wedged open the door and started dragging everything inside. Then she stretched up and turned round—and stared—and stared. . . .

In the middle of the table was something she had never thought to see again. Her rucksack, all her belongings, that she had left behind at the base camp.

Her mouth went dry and she tried to lick her lips. Perhaps—perhaps someone else had returned it; maybe one of the advance party, if they happened to be nearby.

'*Sam!*' He would know. 'Sam!' There was the sound of footsteps outside and she raced to the door throwing it wide. But it wasn't the young native boy standing on the veranda steps—it was Adam Maclean.

It took all Lucy's self-control not to catapult herself into his arms. It was so unbelievable that the person she loved most in all the world should actually be here. He was back in his jungle gear—the khaki trousers and that shirt with all the buttons and tabs. His bronzed skin was shining with a vital glow. He looked as if he had been for a swim in the little lagoon behind the village. He couldn't have been in the river, she would have seen him.

'Do I have to stand out here all evening?' he said dryly, and she stood aside, feeling hot and trembly and hiding her confusion with a shrug.

'I was just surprised, that's all. There was no need for you to bring it back especially.'

'Thanks! Having spent two days hacking my way here, that's just the sort of cheery greeting I can do with.'

They were off. Everything was back to normal. What a fool Lucy had been to have thought it could be any different!

'It's no good blaming me. *I* didn't ask you to come. But if you've got any matches, would you mind lighting that lamp over there.'

He gave it a shake. 'It needs filling.'

'It'll be enough for tonight.' And she picked up one of the boxes and edged her way into the little kitchen.

Adam brought the lamp through and set it on the table. She heaved the box up beside it and began unpacking tins.

'Does the fridge work?' he asked, gazing round in

a wary, uneasy fashion.

'Should do—it's bottled gas. . . . All right, okay,' she added angrily. 'You didn't come all this way to discuss the finer points of my kitchen, such as it is. What do you want? Why did you have to start bothering me again?'

'Bothering you!' He flung the matches on the table, the fridge forgotten. 'You're the one who's bothering me! Night after night. Lying there, seeing you—unable to sleep. Wondering what you're up to. . . .'

'Of all the cheek! Wondering what *I'm* up to! You've got a nerve! Doping me with sleeping tablets so that you could spend another night with your mistress. And don't try and deny it,' she shouted, her blue eyes sparkling with anger and her blonde hair falling over her eyes. 'I saw her coming out of your room that last morning—and you had just had the nerve, the absolute *gall* to ask me to go away with you. Remember?'

'Carmen had come to see if I was up—she knew I had the television interview. . . .'

'Oh, very good. How long did it take you to think that up?'

'Lucy, listen to me.' His face was grim. 'There hasn't been anyone else for me since I met you.'

'You haven't had much opportunity, have you?' she snapped. 'And anyway, I've listened to all I want to hear from you. If you've come to ask me to go to Thailand, then you can think again. Find someone else who's used to sharing her men. I'm not—and I've no intention of starting now!'

'Good! Because I've no intention of sharing you,

either.' All caution and wariness had been cast aside; this was Adam Maclean in his true colours—dangerous and wild. 'So if you'll just keep quiet for a minute and stop making such a fuss.' He grabbed her shoulders and pulled her round to his side of the table.

She struggled.

He shook her. 'For heaven's sake, girl, I haven't come all this way for a stand-up fight. Lucy,' he was practically shouting now, 'Lucy, will you marry me?'

She glared up at him and shouted back. 'No!'

'No?' He seemed thunderstruck as well. 'What do you mean, no?'

Lucy wasn't sure. Lord, what had she done? But he had no right to come barging in here asking her to marry him in that tone of voice. 'I meant, no, I won't marry you,' she said, breaking away. 'I'm sure I can't make it clearer than that.' She marched into the sitting room and he thundered after her.

'Well, don't say I didn't ask you.' He swung the rucksack out of her grasp, and it missed the chair and went crashing to the floor.

'That's it—wreck the place!' Lucy was feeling hysterical now, she didn't know whether to laugh or cry. She backed off, stumbled into the rocking chair, picked up a cushion and threw it at him. And suddenly the fire erupted. She tried to hit him, hurt him, shouting with rage when he easily overpowered her.

'You little witch—kick me, would you?' Only in flip-flops, her toes were bare and it hurt her more than it hurt him. 'Lucy, stop it!' They rocked back against the settee. 'I'm just about at the end of my patience.'

'Let me go—I hate you!' she screamed, and they were tumbling down on to the soft cushions and his lips were savagely searching for hers.

The kiss was fierce, the body contact intimate and revealing. 'I need you, Lucy,' he groaned huskily, 'and I haven't come all this way to be rejected.'

His weight had knocked the wind out of her, and she could feel the raw ache of wanting him gnawing at the pit of her stomach. He was unzipping her jeans, strong, possessive fingers finding the exact spot of her agony. She cried out, excitement and fear pounding through her body like a violent tide.

'Think of it, Lucy—think of it,' he muttered urgently, 'every night like this, if we were married. . . .'

'But we're not going to be married, so there's no point in imagining *anything*,' she sobbed, frantic that she would be unable to stop him—frantic that he would want to stop, even now.

Then there was a noise out on the verandah and he pulled back from her, his face taut and gleaming in the half light.

'They—they must have come for us—for the party,' Lucy gasped somehow. 'We—we've got to go.'

'In a minute,' he snarled, crushing her back into the yielding softness, and giving her a last, passionate, intimate kiss.

'I need you, Lucy,' he whispered again. 'I need you like I've never needed any woman before.' His hands travelled with exquisite agony over her sensitive flesh. 'And, by God, I intend to have you. Tonight. Marriage or no marriage. With your consent—or without it!'

The rest of the evening and long into the night was a heady, unreal pulsating confusion of noise, people, smoke, dancing and music. Lucy and Adam had to sit each side of the chief. They were all togged up in their finery; beautiful headdresses, and a lot of body paint. They had killed a wild pig and a feast of mammoth proportions was spread outside the chief's hut. When it was really dark, the dancing began, the men first, in ornate swirling costumes, and at any other time Lucy would have been fascinated. But tonight she couldn't really concentrate on anything else except Adam's threat.

The drumbeat increased its tempo and a line of women coiled itself into a circle, linking arms and chanting as they stamped and swayed and turned, on and on, in a never-changing rhythm. Piles of food kept appearing in front of Lucy and she picked at this and that, the pork and some fritter things and a tiny banana. Out of the corner of her eyes she could see Adam chatting to the old boy like mad. They were getting on splendidly, plenty of nodding and patting each other on the back. It was doubtful if either of them understood a word of what the other one said. But trust Adam to be able to charm even this old bird out of the trees!

There was some sort of drink passed round as well; it wasn't very pleasant, and as the chanting out front increased, Lucy peered at the dancers and they seemed to hover before her eyes.

She could see that Adam was enjoying it. All that

naked, swinging female flesh. He leant forward to take some fruit, purposefully catching her eye with such a wicked, salacious look that it wasn't far short of rape.

How long did she have to stay here? And then, to her horror, the circle of women parted, two came forward, and with much laughing and giggling she was hauled to her feet.

'No, I can't—I don't know the steps,' but what was the use of protesting in English, and no one was listening, anyway.

Strong female arms twined round her and suddenly Lucy was part of the swaying human chain. She was getting all the steps wrong, being trodden on. Sweat trickled down her back, down her legs. Round and round. . . . Stamp, stamp, twist, bend. . . . The music and chanting became the rhythm of her life. She passed Adam once, twice, he was trying to look as unconcerned as the chief, but she knew that beneath it he was smouldering like the fire. There was no stopping these women, if they hadn't been holding her up, she would have fallen down. She had no will of her own, no resistance. When the drumbeat finally ceased, she staggered back and crumpled in a heap next to Adam.

'Pretty good floor show,' he muttered sideways. 'Pity you weren't dressed for the part.'

She couldn't say anything, she didn't have the breath. The men began smoking, Adam lit up one of his cigars and the chief tried one as well. Perhaps this was the time when the men had their own little chat. Perhaps she could slip away—Adam wouldn't notice.

No such luck. As she edged a little farther from the fire, he turned round and smiled at her sweetly, putting his arm round her shoulders in a friendly fashion. 'Trying to run out?' he asked, his lips still curved charmingly. 'Not yet, my dear Lucy. Not without me.'

Everyone grinned at them, supposing they were having a loving conversation, and it wasn't long afterwards that Adam whispered something to Sam, who translated for his father, and the old man staggered to his feet, everyone else following suit.

'There was no need to break up the party,' Lucy told Adam as he began leading her towards the bungalow. 'I'm not a bit tired,' but all he said was,

'Good.'

She was conscious of every step they took together, the feel of his body as he brushed against her, the warm fingers encircling her arm were touching the sensitive crease of her elbow. She shivered and he responded by tightening his grip.

'Don't think I've changed my mind,' he said, as they began climbing the verandah steps.

The rooms were in darkness and Lucy found the matches and stumbled to the table, groping for the lamp. She had a heady, hazy sense of reality. It was a mixture of excitement, longing and fear. She tried to strike a match, but suddenly Adam was next to her, taking them from her trembling hands, and lighting the wick with steady control. A warm orange glow diffused the darkness, it softened the stern features of his face, it made him intimate, human, extremely desirable.

'Why don't we stop fighting?' he whispered, raising a large hand and gentling back a strand of her hair. 'I want you, my darling,' a tremor ran through him, 'but I want a warm, responsive woman in my arms, not a . . .'

'Fighting, kicking little vixen,' she finished, backing away from the table. She mustn't give in now—she mustn't.

His lips twisted. 'You're not a vixen—you're a witch.'

'And how long would you be satisfied with a responsive little witch?' she managed to ask. 'Six months? A year if I'm lucky? I'm sorry, Adam, it isn't enough.'

'I've already asked you to marry me.'

'If a man wanted something badly enough he might be forced into making all sorts of proposals he might later regret.'

'You think I'm making some idle suggestion? That you're some passing fancy? Lucy, I've never asked anyone to marry me before.' He was getting angry again.

'That's obvious,' she snapped. 'Next time, don't shout!'

'And I'll admit that it just hadn't occurred to me,' he went on firmly. 'Weddings are for families, all that fuss and nonsense—the whole rigmarole.' He left the rest unsaid. 'But have you any idea what it's been like for me this past week? After your accident, I thought things were—good—between us. I wanted you, Lucy, and I nearly went crazy imagining you with Felipe.' He strode towards her and grabbed her arms. 'But I'm not allowing any man the right to touch you ever again. Do you hear me? I want them to know that you are *my wife*.' He pronounced the words with savage eyes. 'And if they come anywhere near you they'll have me to deal with.'

Lucy staggered back under his blast. 'There's more to marriage than ownership,' she insisted.

'Like what?' he roared.

'Like love.'

'Oh!' The fight went out of him—and Lucy died inside. The ultimate commitment and he was backing off. 'I thought you did, you see,' he said, turning away from her and putting his hands in his pockets.

She stared at his back. 'Did what?'

'Love me.' He turned round and shrugged disconsolately, a tight smile not quite curving his lips.

Lucy didn't know what to say, and they stared at each other, her heartbeats increasing in tempo as passion and need gleamed in his eyes. When she didn't respond, he turned away again, his shoulders strained and tight, and she had an uncontrollable urge to press herself against his back.

'I do—I do love you,' she whispered instead. 'I don't think I knew what love was until we met.'

Adam stayed perfectly still for a very long time, then he slowly turned round again and gazed at her in a dream.

'Well then?' he muttered, with a faint sigh.

Lucy had never laid herself so open before. There was so much to gain and so much to lose. Felipe had been right—it took courage. 'But—but it means that you have to love me,' she stumbled quietly.

There was a stunned silence. 'My darling, why else do you imagine I asked you to come away with me?'

'But all those other girl-friends. . . . Carmen told me what used to happen.'

'Did she now?' He was cross but also amused. 'And there were plenty she didn't know about,' he added dryly. Lucy's eyes widened. 'But, darling, don't you see?' Two strides and she was being gathered into his arms. 'They were just girls—for wild weekends,' he shrugged, 'maybe the odd week. But I was asking you to share my life, share my work. And now I'm asking you to be my wife.'

Lucy had discovered love—now she discovered joy. She smiled, coiling her arms around his neck and nestling provocatively.

'I see,' she taunted, the old dull ache returning, demonstrating the need that only he could satisfy.

He slid strong hands up and down her sides. 'Will you,' he prompted, 'will you come back to England with me once my expedition is over—as my wife?'

'Yes, please,' she whispered, undoing a shirt button and kissing his chest. 'If that's what you want.'

He smiled, liking what she was doing to him, but determined to have his say. 'I want you with me, Lucy, now and always. There'll be no staying on in Brazil. The place for my wife is with me.'

'Try and keep me away!' Another button came undone and she spread her palms over the smooth hardness beneath.

He gasped, and she felt his tightening body respond. 'I'm not sure how long marriages take to arrange out here,' he muttered, making his own invasion of her shirt. 'Two or three weeks, probably.'

She began nibbling his ear. 'You could be right.'

'And I don't want to wait that long. I want you now, my darling—tonight. . . .'

'As you said,' she reminded him, 'with my consent—or without it.'

His dark, searching eyes turned her soul to liquid fire. 'Which is it to be?' he whispered.

'Which would please you most?' she heard herself say.

'You little witch!' And suddenly they were smiling, laughing, clinging to each other, and Lucy could feel tears of happiness pouring down her cheeks. Adam pulled her shirt out of her jeans. 'You're very hot. Would you like a shower?' And when she nodded, he added, 'So would I.'

With mounting excitement they began undressing each other. Lucy's fingers trembled; this couldn't really be happening, yet there was no shame, just an unbelievable longing and fascination at the magnificent splendour of his body.

His face shone with the joy of their discovery. He picked her up, holding her high in the air, simply for the exquisite pleasure of sliding her down the long, hard, sensuous length of him. Then he carried her to the little shower room and the water ran in unison over their mingling limbs.

'You're so beautiful—I don't think I can wait much longer.' There was an urgency in his voice now, and a terrifying thrill ran through her.

'Adam—Adam, I think there's something you should know,' she whispered secretly.

'Later!' The word was a husky groan deep in his throat.

'No—please—it's important.' But he wouldn't

listen, he was kissing her, wrapping her up in a towel, and carrying her towards the little narrow bed. His skin smelt fresh, damp, but they hadn't used soap and there was a musky maleness about him that she found inexplicably stimulating.

'Adam, it's about Felipe,' she implored, as he eased her back against the pillows and began rubbing her dry.

His face tightened and a muscle down his cheek pulsated wildly. 'Not now—I don't want to know.'

'But you must!' She could feel anger and passion beneath his trembling fingers. If he thought that she was used to men—and if he was angry—like now . . . Fear momentarily closed her eyes. 'Adam, you have to know. Felipe and I didn't—I mean, I'm not his mistress.' She stared up at the hard, implacable face, and slowly, very slowly, the savageness died away.

'You mean that?' But he knew that she did, and a triumphant joy and satisfaction seared his face. Then he closed his eyes and for a moment she saw all the misery and pain he had suffered that week. How much he must truly love her—almost as much as she loved him. 'Why?' he muttered eventually, like a drowning man.

'Because—because you had Carmen, I suppose.'

He sighed. 'And that other fellow in England, what was his name?'

'John? No, I didn't sleep with John, either. I didn't love him, you see. I've never loved anyone but you.' As she said it, he eased the towel from between them and snaked sensuously on top of her. The hard strength of his body was all the rousing she needed, and her back arched instinctively, inviting his possession.

Then the face of the man she loved changed to almost smug self-satisfaction. 'So I was right,' he said, 'all that driving myself mad with wanting you on the boat—frightened to touch you in case . . .'

'In case of what?' she asked mischievously.

'In case I wouldn't be gentle enough, my sweet white virgin.'

'And will you now?'

He began kissing her. 'To begin with.'

'Only to begin with?' she teased.

His eyes ignited with a dangerouss fire. 'Oh yes, only to begin with. You'll see. . . .'

ROMANCE